I0736741

Rogues and Heroes

A Short Story Collection

Sabrina Chase

Cover art by Les Petersen
ISBN-13: 978-0-940006-25-3

"Our Man in Basingstoke" first published in *Fiction River: Spies* (2019) WMG Press

"Inspection" first published in The Bureau of Substandards Annual Report (2013)

"A Day Spent Fishing" first published 2012

"The Correct Way to Fill Out Form PCR-103-u" first published 2012, also appears in *The Bureau of Substandards Annual Report* (2013)

"Crossing Over the River" first published in *Pulphouse Magazine* issue #4 2018

"Coyote and the Amazing Herbal Formula" first published 2012, also appeared in *Pulphouse Magazine* issue #0 (2017)

"Inscription" first published 2015

CONTENTS

Also by Sabrina Chase

THE SEQUOYAH TRILOGY:
The Long Way Home
Raven's Children
Queen of Chaos

GUARDIAN'S COMPACT
The Last Mage Guardian
Dragonhunters

ARGONAUTS TRILOGY
The Scent of Metal
One Blood
Soul Code

Firehearted
Jinxers
The Bureau of Substandards Annual Report

ACKNOWLEDGMENTS

Many thanks to editor Patrick Richardson who fought manfully against the flood of commas, proofreader Roger "I see dead quotemarks" Ivie, and artist Les Peterson who was told to "go nuts" with the cover design…and did.

ONE MORE THING

It was just another dusty warehouse in the dusty industrial dome of Desy sector. It didn't even have a pressure door or a holosign or even a secondary dome. Inathka was sure it was the right place, though, because two muscular offworlders were hanging around near the main entrance and they hadn't gone anywhere for nearly an hour. Why have guards if it wasn't important?

She took a deep breath and walked straight up to them as if she'd been there a hundred times before. "Heard might be infotech work," she said, as one of the heavies lounged over to block her way. She knew better than to mention Garcen up front.

The heavy gave her a contemptuous look, spat at the ground, then took a pull on his hydration tube. "If'n was, ye'd get call. If'n ye good 'nuf."

"I'm best. Don't spew my sched, but happens I got some free cycles for innerestin' work and *dos* load." Inathka shrugged. "Boss-man hear I offer and got turnaway, might go bad, personal-like." She gave the heavy half a smile, like she was being mannered and thinking twice about it.

It was a pure gamble, but it worked. The heavy called in, listened a bit, then waved at his buddy to open the door. Inathka followed the heavy down a network of shadowy corridors. She could smell hydraulic fluid, acrid and oily, when they went past one door. Shouldn't be anything needing that in this dome, at least nothing legit. Another good sign.

Garcen didn't look like a fixer. Big guy, a little soft here and there like a heavy that didn't need to fight much any more; ordinary coveralls with stains and dirt just like everybody else doing hard work, Inathka included. He was talking to a small group that looked like they might be office types maybe, but not high-up ones. When the heavy brought Inathka in, Garcen glanced over with a scowl.

"You the best, huh? Best of yer school-group maybe, kid. Never seen ya. What's the name?"

Inathka shook her head. "Yeh, like I sign off on the invoices," she said with scorn. "Mebbe should notice, you *never* heard of me. Tell you something, if'n ya think." Inwardly she shrunk. Getting mouthy wasn't real healthy, but they'd expect a bit if she was real top line. Plus, she had to dodge the awkward questions, like whether she was still in school. Technically she was, or rather a limited feedback script pretending to be her was online and doing her interactives.

Garcen snorted. "I also never heard of nobodies. So, you'd take on any wandering dip with need? How's I gonna figgure you, no-name?"

"I gives a free taste, 'course. What you want done, only best can do? I hands over proof, you hire for the big job." She could see he was thinking about it. Free work would let him check her out for little risk, and she'd heard he was cheap where he could be.

He grinned, and not friendly-like. "Sure. You get me the full Indris cargo schedule, current. Down to the crate data. Bring me that, you hired."

Inathka narrowed her eyes. "You don't care when?" Maybe she could do this at home, which would be a plus.

Garcen waved his hand at the group of maybe-office people. "Before they do." Now everybody was grinning. Inathka kept her face blank and inwardly ran through all her curse words and invented a few new ones. Of course someone else would have heard the same rumors. Of course Garcen would already have somebody in mind. Nothing to do but play along, and hope she got the data before the school found the script.

Outside, Inathka walked away like she was on off time as long as she was still in view of the heavies, but once she had turned the corner she sprinted for the fence with the hole in the chain-link. From there she climbed to the ledge where she had observed Garcen's building earlier, sank to a crouch, and though hard.

Time was the limiting factor. The others had their gear; the wrist units alone were more than her monthly pay. There was a team of four, and she was on her own. The snoop gear she has was not nearly as good and more importantly was hidden two domes away. It would take over an hour to retrieve it. Getting caught with snoop gear was dangerous, especially when she was planning on actually doing something with it, which was why she had hidden it in the first place.

No, she just had to work with what she had with her; a generic comm unit, a broken screwdriver, and a basic set of data leads she'd forgotten were in her coverall pockets. Her father had given her an ultimatum. Get a job, or get sent to the welfare barracks when she came of age. Of course, with her grades the only jobs in Desy were the back-breaking, dangerous, and low-paying ones—nothing with data or infotech. She had to get off-planet and a job with Garcen was the only way.

Not long after she took up her post, the four infotechs left Garcen's building. They didn't look happy. She followed them from the ledge until that ran out, jumping down and finding a way up to the next vantage point until she figured out where they were headed—xthe offices of Idris shipping lines. That made sense. Garcen wasn't after the ship schedule; that was publicly available and the data stored in the common core for the data net. The stuff he was after was the crate index. What cargo was going on which ship on what day, and what the crate code was. The crates all looked the same, varying only in size, and had an encoded chip. Only the master index knew what cargo was in a particular crate, and she was pretty sure she knew which cargo Garcen was interested in. He couldn't steal them all without being noticed, so he needed the index.

Since she knew their destination she could speed

ahead. She had a bad moment when the gang started up for the same roof she was on, but they weren't looking for her. They were headed for the comm hutch, where the secure network for Idris connected up with the rest of the dome systems. Inathka watched glumly, making a list of all the hi-pro gear they had and she didn't. Multicycle electronic key, for one. That got them inside the hutch. It wasn't built to be roomy, so she got to see the rest of the gear as they pulled it out and handed it to the guy inside. Cable induction sleeve, with an attached slot for a data tab.

The gang finished up, did a quick search to pick up any stray sign of their presence, and left—unfortunately remembering to check that the hutch door was latched before they did. Inathka waited a few minutes to make sure they were really gone before she moved from her hiding place.

Great. She knew what they were doing now, and she could do damnall to stop them. Idris did a daily secure backup of their internal data. The gang was going to intercept it with the induction sleeve. There must be a filter set to only pick up the crate invoice or otherwise it would take a whole cube to capture the upload. They would record it right there, and then come back and get the data tab the next day. Slick.

She prowled around the data hutch, making sure she could not be seen from the street. From what she'd seen of the interior of the hutch, the main conduit didn't come straight up from below, but ran horizontally along the roof. She took out her screwdriver and started digging. Of course the screwdriver couldn't break through the roof or the conduit underneath—she was just making a pool for the solvent she'd seen when she was hiding. It was airseal solvent, and burned pretty hot once you got it started. Somebody must have left it doing a repair and forgot it.

First she had to wait for the data transfer. She didn't know exactly when that happened, but presumably during dark cycle when there was less activity. So she waited, huddled on the roof and hoping she'd guessed right. Then light started to appear again, and she shifted her stiff limbs into action. Inathka filled the little pool with solvent right where she needed it, then did a careful leak to the convincing location to leave the solvent container. Then it was just a matter of stripping some loose wire, finding a power outlet, and giving the solvent a spark.

The solvent flared up, nearly singing her eyebrows.

Inathka poured a little more solvent to keep it going and scrambled hastily off the roof with the wire.

Sure enough, first an Idris employee showed up, yelled, and reappeared with fire supression gear. Not long after that a repair tech showed up. As she had hoped, the damage was extensive enough he kept having to go back to his cart for more gear. It was easy for her to time his trips, slip in, and grab the data tab.

First she copied the data to her phone. A quick look told her it was exactly what she was looking for. Then, with a little effort, she copied random data back onto the tab. One more repair tech trip, and she put the corrupted tab back in place.

Just for fun, she went in the Idris front office and purchased a full Idris shipping schedule, claiming she was working for an exporter. It came on an Idris-branded datatab. Using a public kiosk, she copied the crate invoice over the schedule. She didn't want her trick stealing the data to be too obvious, and she sure didn't want to hand over her phone. Even a clean phone would have traceable data on it.

Inathka didn't want to show up too much in advance of the gang, so she waited until she saw a familiar face near the Idris building before heading to

Garcen. The guards let her in without comment. Garcen wasn't delighted to see her, but she was gratified by the flash of surprise in his eyes when she laid the datatab on his desk.

"You got in first. Didja get it right? Looks OK, but I'm gonna see what the others got first." He leaned back in his chair, giving her an appraising stare. "You so good, but you don't gotta name? Think I shoulda heard a somebody like that, mebbe." Inathka shrugged. Half an hour later the gang came in, strutting. The confident walk stumbled a bit when they saw her, and she thought one of the gang had a distinctly worried expression that slipped out now and then.

Garcen took their datatab and scanned it. His face darkened. "What the hell is this garbage? Look at it! That's useless!"

The gang leader took a look at the screen and his jaw dropped. "Na, it weren't like that when we got it, I swear! We did it all slim-side, real."

"The fire..." the worried one muttered, eyes going wide as she finally made the connection. "It scrambled the data. It wasn't our fault!"

"So, I got a job?" Inathka kept all signs of triumph to herself. No point in getting the others madder than they were already, and she needed to act like this was no big deal.

Garcen's expression grew hard. "Not so fast. I gotta get a better feel for what you can do, since I can't ask around about you, no-name. You gotta do one more thing, you wanna work for me. You gotta bring me this crate." A thick finger stabbed down at the display. "Think you can?"

Inathka stifled a spurt of temper. She'd done exactly what he'd asked, and now she had to do more? Yeah, she was desperate for the work but not desperate to be taken for a ride. "Sure I can. Prep won't be cheap, though."

"Why? You got your gear, doncha?"

"Yep. And you got money. I said one free sample; you got it. Piecework ain't my style, but if that's how you wanna do it, I'm agreeable." Inathka took deep, slow breaths. Show no fear. That was hard with Garcen looking like he'd like to kill her.

"Like I'd give you money, now you know the hit." He snorted. "I got some stuff in the back. You use that. Bring me the crate, you got the job."

One of the gang reluctantly showed her the back room. It was full of all kinds of broken and shabby crap.

Boxes, crates, emergency lights on stands, the bottom half of a repair mech, even an old jitney with faded lettering on the side. Inathka studied the room, frowning, until the guy was out of sight down the hall. She darted after him, soundless, pulling out her screwdriver and pulling on the broken handle until it came off.

The door to Garcen's room was closed, but she was expecting that. She took the hollow screwdriver handle and put it to the edge where the seal was loose, and put her ear against the handle.

"...you sure? Nothin'?"

"I scan all over. Just some cheap disposaphone, got that number, but it don't go nowhere. She don't got any ID."

Garcen's voice. "She know about me, right? She know about the cargo. She know her job better than you idiots!"

"We had it right, just that fire screwed it up," whined one of the gang. "So she got lucky. You gonna hire her when you don't know who she is? Could be a nose, come from offworld even, hired by one a the *combina*."

"No, I ain't gonna hire her. I don't hire people think they smarter than me. But you lot, you not smarter than *anyone*. So, here's what we do. She's gonna get that crate for us, and then you grab it and do for her, right? Do the drop to the blues. Then nobody gonna be looking for us."

This was followed by laughter, strained a bit around the edges. Inathka heard footsteps approaching and ran back to the storeroom before anyone saw her.

Fuming, she considered her options. If she stole the crate, she still wouldn't have a job, which was the whole point. She could give up and go back to the habitat dome, but that would waste all the time she'd put in here and she still would be stuck with a crap job in a few months no matter what she did. What could she do with what she had?

The jitney kept tugging at her attention. The lettering was hard to make out, but looked like "Transport", and a logo. More rummaging found her a coverall with a nametag, a package of new plastifiber cartons, a dome directory, and an old, insulated lunchbag with "Tenebris Security" on it. The cargo was scheduled to be on a ship lifting in four days, so she had some time to prepare.

First, she plugged the jitney in to charge up the battery. Then she looked up delivery services and a public schedule of cargo ships arriving at the port. She made up a bunch of packages, filling them with useless junk from the storeroom and giving them random local addresses, then tossing them about in the dirtiest, most dusty corners until they looked like they had been in a cargo hold for weeks.

She loaded the jitney with the packages and an empty crate, changed into the coverall, and headed for the port. The Idris office was easy to find. She kept going past it, though, stopping at other shipping offices and never going inside, but tossing a package into the empty crate at every stop, looking industrious and tired. Near break time she arranged to be back at the Idris office. Several other jitney drivers were also stopped. She got out her lunch bag, pretending to eat while looking around. Yep, one driver was taking a quick nap. She got out and headed towards the public facilities, but before she got there ducked down and snuck back to the sleeping Idris driver. She nabbed two packages from the outside of the jitney cargo bin and snuck back, tossing one in the crate. Then she stepped inside the office.

"Hey," she said. An older man was inside. "I have this for dropoff." It was already labeled and stamped, from a firm with an account.

"They make you work through your break?" the man asked. His nametag said "Erdan".

Inathka gave a wan smile. "Yeah. Just like you, huh?" He took the package with a grunt. "Hey, you want one? Vendabot gave me two by mistake." She held out one of the cracker packages.

"Thanks. Can't even get out to the vendabot, stupid schedule. 'preciate it."

Inathka waved and trudged out.

Her next stop was near the ship docks. She found a place to hide the jitney, took off the coverall, and snooped. The ship she wanted, as she had seen from the arrivals, had just come in. Cargo was being offloaded. It was a small Inner Systems freighter, used for short runs on "sealed" worlds with open docks as opposed to larger freighters that required stations, and didn't land on planets. All the hatches opened from the outside.

Having seen what she needed, Inathka hopped an empty garbage tube container and snuck back into the habitat dome. If her plan was to work, she'd need her ID and her tools. She left innocuous messages for her parents, grabbed a few tabs of diuretic forgotten from her grandfather's last visit, and returned to the port dome. She hid her ID and some of the tools on the upper surface of a beam that was so thick with dust she knew nobody ever went there. By now it was the start of a new workday, and she dropped off the second purloined package at Idris. Her buddy Erdan was there, as she had hoped, and she waved.

She kept up the deception for the next few days, keeping an eye on the cargo ship, sneaking in her bogus packages to the regular Idris jitneys coming from the docks and "picking up" expected deliveries or "delivering" other packages headed to Idris that she'd intercepted. She'd learned Erdan had been married twice, had a daughter close to her in age, liked fish-flavored crackers, and hated working late.

She'd also learned the cargo ship was planning to lift off immediately after loading. The crate Garcen wanted her to grab was due to be delivered tomorrow. She'd driven by the ship several times and eaten her lunch at the communal area nearby, and had chatted with the crew.

That night, she took her tools and did some careful work on one of the cargo doors that had been left unsecured. Now, it was unsecured and wouldn't seal, but that wouldn't be noticed until they opened and then closed it again.

One more stop in the morning. Picking up another fake package, slipping in another one, and a "mislabled" cracker package, that was fish instead of cheese and she knew her buddy Erdan liked them. It was dosed with the emetic.

Inathka sped off to her favorite ship-watching place to watch the show she had set into action. First, the secure cargo delivery showed up, all nice and proper. It didn't say secure delivery, of course. That would be giving it away. But if you knew what to look for, the delivery people were all fit and some had suspicious bulges where a gun might be worn. The crates were loaded. No excitement yet. But then the crew tried to close all the hatches, and the careful procedure started coming unstuck. One refused to close properly. With a great deal of yelling, it was clear a repair needed to happen, and the door was still wide open, and it was late local time. Now she had to time things properly.

They couldn't leave the valuable crate on the ship, unsecured. They had to get it back to the secure facility as soon as possible, but they couldn't advertise it was a valuable crate, either. The sensible thing would be to hand it back to the Idris office, which would know what to do.

Only the late hour Idris employee was not feeling well. And since he didn't know the crate was valuable, he had no problem letting that nice jitney girl take the crate back for him, on her way home, so he could stay in the back office and sleep a bit. Just to make sure no awkward questions got asked, he loaned her an Idris namepatch for her coverall. They'd never see the jitney from inside, would they?

Inathka grinned wildly as she zoomed off in her jitney. She had the crate. She'd even delivered it to Idris, admittedly without the original contents, which were in the old empty crate she'd taken from the storeroom, and tossed in some more junk on top to conceal the contents even if the lid was taken off. She drove the jitney back to Garcen's place and parked it back inside the storeroom, and moved the crate to the side, covering it with a tarp. Then she took off the Idris nametag and left it stuck inside the crate.

"I got it, and they don't even know it's gone," she said to Garcen. "I switched out crates, taking the real code and putting it on an empty crate, and had the real one shipped to a mail drop for pickup. All you gotta do is take this keytab and pick it up. No trail."

The gang looked uneasily at Garcen. He didn't say

anything for a while, looking at the keytab in his hand, which had the address printed on the side. "Yeah. Good work." He tossed the key back at her. "You got the job. Now go pick it up and bring it here."

Inathka smiled brightly. "Sure thing, boss." She ignored the muttering and angry looks from the gang, and didn't start running until the door closed behind her. Now timing was crucial.

She pushed the jitney as fast as it would go, heading for the port docks. Yep, some of the crew were waiting at the common area for the repair techs. She parked the jitney and walked towards them, cultivating a worried look and looking over her shoulder a few times.

"Um, I'm really sorry to bother you, and I know it's an imposition, but could I borrow your ship comm?"

"Why? You've got a local comm right there," one of the crew pointed out, correctly.

"Yeah. Um, they can be traced, you know? I need to call the police, and...and the person I'd be calling about would take it bad. Real bad." She rubbed her throat and swallowed. "I can't risk it."

That got her attention. "Police?" They looked at each other. "I think we can swing that. If you don't mind us listening?"

She shook her head vehemently. "Nah, you're going off world, he won't bother you."

They took her inside, and Inathka secretly reveled in the novelty of the ship interior. This is what she wanted. Over the comm she gave the police a frightened description of seeing some shady people in a jitney with the Idris company logo, people she didn't recognize and she was familiar with the team since she worked cargo too. "And they opened the crate, and they took the stuff inside and handed it to a man. I heard one say elamantium is real pricy, no? The man yelled at them to shut up. And then they drove off and he took the stuff inside the building." She gave the address, making sure her voice was still shaking.

The crew members were gaping at her. "Elamantium? Are you sure?" Inathka nodded.

More calls were made. Idris first confirmed the presence of the crate, then that the crate was empty. Then that the police had raided Garcen's place and found the contents, arresting him.

"Wow. You have totally earned the reward," Miren, one of the crew, said. "And it's a percentage of the value, so you really did well."

"Oh, is elamantium expensive?"

One of the others nodded. "That crate they tried to grab? Five hundred thousand Eurodollar, minimum."

Inathka gasped, clapped her hands over her mouth, and bit down on her tongue, hard. The tears spilled over her cheeks.

"Oh no. Oh no. I'm dead."

Miren bent over her, concerned. "Why? What's wrong?"

"If it's that expensive, one of the big *combinas* is involved. I messed up their grab. They're going to *kill* me. I thought if I just told the police, it would be all over..." she sobbed. "I gotta get off planet, but I don't have any money. What am I going to do?"

"But the reward..."

Miren punched him in the arm. "She has to stay to collect it, right? Give her name and stuff. Bad guys would find out, right?"

The quiet guy stood up. "Hey. The reward comes from Idris, right? And she needs off-planet, right? How about we hire her, just this trip. Idris can route the funds to the next stop. I'm sure we can find something for her to do for that long."

"Yeah, that'll work," Miren agreed. "So, tell me, what can you do? We don't got jitneys on board."

"Well," Inathka sniffled, "I've been studying data security...."

OUR MAN IN BASINGSTOKE

The prisoner showed no sign of fear when brought into Sir Almsley's office. On the contrary—he appeared to consider the experience a high treat, despite muddy trousers and bramble-scratches on his round, beaming face. He appeared to be no more than nine years old, and was looking about with great interest and absolutely no embarrassment despite Sergeant Ross's firm grip on his collar.

"It's the second time 'e's tried to get in," Ross stated. "Willins sent him off from the front gate yesterday." While Ross maintained a stony demeanor, the fact that he was barely moving his jaw when he spoke informed those who knew him well that his volcanic temper was under considerable strain. "I found 'im by the stables just now."

Sir Almsley sighed and removed his pince-nez, placing it on the scattered piles of papers on his desk before rubbing his aching head. "Did he use the front gate today as well?" Private Willins was...not entirely reliable as a guard, but he and Ross had decided he would cause the least harm there. A decision they might have to revisit.

"I found a hole under the fence in the forest," the boy said proudly. "I think it was a badger's." His wandering gaze snagged on an antique bronze statuette of Ganesha. "I say...is that a mystic idol from a hidden jungle kingdom guarded by fanatic dervishes in black masks covered with jewels?"

It took Sir Almsley a moment to collect his stunned thoughts. "Er, no. I bought it in a bazaar in Bombay." He stifled an impulse to apologize for this apparent lapse in good taste. "Do you have any excuse for your trespassing, young man? We are engaged in important war work here and do not have time for interruptions."

The boy nodded vigorously. "That's why I've come. To volunteer! And to see the secret underground base."

Sir Almsley's headache escalated to sharp, stabbing

pain behind his eyes. He had quite enough to worry about without scrubby schoolboys being added to the mix. "There are absolutely no secret underground bases anywhere on the grounds," he snapped. It was something of a sore point that the War Office had given him a difficult task and hardly anything to do it with. He hadn't even been allotted extra petrol rations—or, more importantly, competent guards.

"I know you have to say that to people, in case they are German spies," the boy said, unabashed. "I saw that in *The Spies of the Red Hand*. Ripping film, even if it did have some mushy romance stuff in it. But you can *see* I'm not German, can't you? My father is with the 47th Berkshires. You could ring them up and ask! My name is Peter Tilling. They sent me up from London on account of the air raids." A frown darkened his sunny expression. "I could've helped if they let me stay. Mum did, even though all she seems to do with the Air Raid wardens is stand around wearing an armband and serve coffee. *I* can do that, and I'm not quite ten!"

Although he knew he would regret it, Sir Almsley felt compelled to ask. "Why did you think there was an underground base here?"

"Before the war my father worked for a mining

company. He let me push the detonator once for a tunnel! I heard an explosion a few days ago and there aren't mines here, just cows. So of *course* it had to be for a secret base! Do you have mechanized mole machines? You know, the ones that travel underground." Peter dug out a large and rather grubby notebook from under his shirt. "See, I had ideas to make 'em even better. I thought of a way to make a periscope for one. That way they can stay underground and not be seen. Like a submarine, you know. Then you can win the war and my father can come home."

Sir Almsley's fascinated gaze fell on the page young Peter had presented for his edification. A quite detailed drawing of some kind of armored cigar-shaped vehicle with treads and a corkscrew nose was shown, and a device with nested pipes and a long auger that appeared to create the hole for the periscope. He replaced his pince-nez to examine it more closely.

"I say, that is quite clever." He looked up at Ross, bemused. "*Do* we have these...underground mole machines?" Modern life moved far too fast for him. It seemed incredible, but he had thought the aeroplane a hoax at first and now his youngest son was *flying* one of the damned things.

"Never heard of 'em." Sergeant Ross's tone implied if they did exist, he didn't approve of that fact.

"It was in an illustrated number of *Stupendous Stories*," Peter informed them. "I got *lots* of ideas from that, and *Thrilling Zeppelin Tales. Boys Own Adventure* has ripping stories too, but I can't think how finding lost civilizations in Brazil can help fight the war." His bright eyes looked eagerly at Ross and Sir Almsley, as if they might have noticed something he'd missed.

Ross scratched his head. "'ere, lad. If they sent you up from London who took you in? Shouldn't you be helping them, then? Won't they be worried if they can't find you?"

Peter rolled his eyes and sighed heavily. "It's a *farm*. They don't have anything to read, or even a wireless! Well, when I got there I tried to train the cows to attack on command. That would be useful, wouldn't it? Bet that would surprise any German invaders! But the farmer just got angry and locked me in my room. So I climbed down a tree and decided to find something else to do." Peter did not appear to hold a grudge over his treatment. "All the posters say England Needs You. I know I'm not old enough to join up, but there has to be *something* I can do to help."

There was just a touch of wistfulness in the boy's voice that caused a sympathetic twinge in Sir Almsley. Hadn't he done much the same thing? Between his age and the lingering ill-health from Indian fevers that had cut short his youthful military career, he had little to offer personally in the service of King and country. His two sons were, of course, serving with courage and it weighed heavily on him that he could do nothing to assist them as they went in harm's way.

Then he had heard through an old friend in government how someone had made their house and grounds available for some hush-hush project—Bletchley Park, as he recalled. No one had any idea exactly what they did there, but many clever fellows from Oxford were going there and seemed to be quite busy. The house had been far too quiet with the absence of his sons, and his wife had been dead many years. No one would be troubled if the government moved in, and he could observe and perhaps talk to the clever fellows and find a way to be of further assistance.

The reality was far otherwise. The government had accepted his offer of the use of Dunglenn and grounds, and a chap from the War Office contacted him about what he had termed "covert operations." Sir Almsley had been under the vague impression that this was somehow connected to hunting, which he remembered enjoying in his youth. But then to his shock he was informed that this was their new programme to develop...what was their phrase for it? "Espionage doctrine, techniques, and equipment."

Sir Almsley was of a generation that firmly believed gentlemen did not read each other's mail, and most certainly did not engage in what could only be described as skullduggery. While he appreciated times had changed and the Hun certainly did not have such nice notions, he was at a loss on what he could do to assist.

He'd also thought that the government would bring their own people in to run the thing, and he would merely observe from the periphery. Instead they had put him in charge, and instead of clever fellows from Oxford he had been given a store of dynamite and old ammunition in calibres no longer used by the military, and a group of soldiers that Sergeant Ross had apostrophized as a human scrap metal drive. He suspected a few had even engaged in poaching and other illicit activities.

Now he was expected to report on what he and his

miniscule team had accomplished, which wasn't much. Certainly, they had learned how to detonate dynamite but no clever tricks had occurred to anyone in the process. He anticipated his upcoming visit to Headquarters with utter gloom. He had hoped to plead for more resources, but given how little the Dunglenn project had produced the danger was the War Office would write the whole thing off as a failure.

Until then, however, he had a duty. He remembered enough of his military training to know an officer's duty included supporting the morale of his men by example. He paged through Peter's notebook, pausing to study a few of the diagrams and capture loose pages that escaped the covers. "Your enthusiasm is admirable," Sir Almsley said. "England needs us all to do our utmost for victory, does it not? I am afraid I have no position suited to your talents...but perhaps you would be willing to leave your notebook with me? I promise will give it full consideration." Peter nodded vigorously, eyes glowing with delight. Then Sir Almsley was inspired to a very mild deception. For the lad's own good, and Sir Almsley's peace of mind. "But I must ask you not to come here again—unless we contact you, of course." That had been a narrow escape. "There are spies everywhere now, and what if they followed you and uncovered...our secrets?" *How I dearly wish we had any worth stealing.*

"Oh!" Peter blinked. "Gosh. No, that would ruin everything! I'm staying at Hereston Farm, near the village of Basingstoke. Well, they say it is a village but it doesn't have much. I don't expect they have any spies, either."

"Nevertheless, we must take every precaution," Sir Almsley said firmly. "Sergeant Ross, will you escort young Mr. Tilling to the, er, badger hole? So he may return without being observed." He hoped his meaningful gaze was correctly interpreted as instructing him to block that means of entry in future.

With a cheery wave, Peter left under official escort and Sir Almsley returned to the hopeless muddle on his desk. But only minutes later there came a knock and the information that the car waited to take him to the station.

His trip to London, and he still had not prepared his report! In a panic, Sir Almsley stuffed as many of the papers as he could fit in a large leather satchel. Perhaps he could work on the train—and in any event, it would serve to show he'd not been slacking.

With his poor health travel always fatigued him,

and so did the frenetic activity of London despite the gloom of the blackout restrictions and wartime rationing. Far too many buildings had been reduced to piles of rubble, making travel difficult, and people on the street looked tired and drawn. Everyone carried a small case with a gas mask. But even through his fatigue he noticed the people at the War Office seemed abstracted, paying only cursory attention to what he was saying. He'd hoped that perhaps he could make a case for more resources, or at least a few men with all their limbs and no prison records, but his time with the department heads was cut short by some urgent issue and he was handed over to a polite but bored young man with pale eyes who introduced himself as George Smythe.

"It's odds on we'll get a pasting tonight," Smythe said, looking at the clock in the meeting room. "Bomber's moon, don't you know. You should think about leaving before dark, sir."

"But my files...I haven't shown you any of them."

A faint glimmer in the pale eyes. "You may leave them with me if you like, sir, and I will hand them on. With respect, I think you would find the air raid shelters rather uncomfortable—and of course, the bombing makes it hard to sleep."

Sir Almsley accepted defeat, and handed over his files with a heavy heart. It was marginally preferable to be informed via letter that there was nothing of use, versus being told so in person.

He heard nothing for several days after his return to Dunglenn. After ten days he resolutely sent a telegram to inquire, which did not elicit a response.

The next day, however, a nervous lieutenant appeared at his door, with a startling letter from the War Office.

"Stolen?" Sir Almsley stared at the lieutenant, who mopped his brow.

"Yes sir. We only noticed once we got your telegram. You see, Smythe never mentioned he had your files so we'd thought you'd taken them back with you, and with the confusion of the bombing.... well, once we started asking around Smythe vanished. We...we think he was a spy, sir."

Sir Almsley's first reaction was, strangely, satisfaction. The stolen files were certainly not crucial to the war effort, and had exposed a dangerous spy in the heart of the War Office before real damage was done.

"Bad show, that," he said finally. The lieutenant was still nervous.

"There's more, sir. We, well, of course we have our own spies. Without saying how we know this, we've learned the Germans seem quite worked up about something in those files. They mentioned Dunglenn specifically, sir. They've been observed driving iron rods into the ground around some of their more sensitive installations, huge numbers of them. Iron they can scarcely spare. And they've been sending messages back and forth about what we think is called a...*Erdepanzer*, or earth tank. We were hoping you could tell us more."

Sir Almsley removed his pince-nez, distantly amazed that his hands did not shake. He shifted the papers on his desk until he found it, a ratty notebook. The page with the mole machine was indeed missing—and thinking back, he recalled how some of the pages had come loose, and how he'd been in such a hurry he'd simply gathered the papers on his desk to take with him.

A daring plan suddenly emerged from the depths of his mind, awe-inspiring in its audacity. With a single piece of paper, young Peter Tilling had sown chaos and confusion in the German war machine, making them waste rare and valuable resources that could no longer be used to make tanks and weapons.

And he could never confess that a nine year old boy

had done it. Not if he intended to do it again.

"Not to worry," he said, and leaned back. "This little incident is an excellent proof of one of the cunning ideas this project devised. A very clever fellow came up with that—a trifle eccentric, perhaps—but I saw the potential. That was a deliberate ploy. There are no *Erdepanzers*, but we made them think there were, eh? And all to our advantage in the end. Jerry is running around defending against something that doesn't exist. Quite a cost-effective stratagem, what?"

Sir Almsley was quite gratified by the lieutenant's gaping expression. "Sir! You did this... on purpose?"

Not yet inured to the demands of spycraft, he could only nod to give the wrong impression rather than voice an outright lie. "And there are more where that came from." He tossed over the notebook. "The War Office will doubtless know where they can be used to best effect. Where you think you might have a spy or two, eh?"

"That's bloody brilliant, sir! Er, pardon my language." The lieutenant stood. "I'd best get back immediately. What a relief! We thought we'd cocked it up proper. Shall I take this?" He held up Peter's notebook.

Sir Almsley nodded gravely. "Guard it well."

#

"This come wi' the mail, sir." The soldier was completely unidentifiable, in black clothes and with grease smeared over his face. He held a brown paper parcel, and placed it on the table in the sunny side parlor.

"Ah, our research materials have arrived. Thank you. Any luck? It's nearly noon." Sir Almsley, amused, observed the man's jaw tighten.

"He's a slippery one, and no mistake. We'll earn that brandy yet, sir!" The soldier gave a determined nod and left.

The package contained the latest issues of several booklets with lurid covers promising adventure and excitement. Sir Almsley observed the time wanted but five minutes to twelve, and then saw the sash of one window lift slightly, followed shortly by Peter wriggling through the opening. He had several twigs and a small feather stuck in his hair, and a wide grin on his face.

"They've gotten loads better, Sir Almsley! I nearly didn't make it in time!"

Sir Almsley smiled. "You've been an excellent trainer. I've gotten word from Sergeant Ross, by-the-bye. He tells me his new unit has made excellent use of what he learned from you about sneaking to great purpose." And since the commandos were doing amazing things in the war, this earned his project even more credit. He was told that the Dunglenn training program had become very much in demand in certain departments of the army. "I daresay they will earn their prize of brandy in a few days."

Young Peter's skill in getting into places he shouldn't had been given new purpose in the training. A discreet visit to the farm, with a cover story of "needing a boy to help the groundskeeper," had covered matters on that end with no one the wiser and the farmer relieved. Ross had come up with the idea of the competition as an incentive to the men. Every day, Peter set out from the farm at the same time with the goal of getting inside the house before noon without detection. Once the soldiers caught him, Sir Almsley awarded them a bottle from his private stock.

"We have new material to research," he said, indicating the pulp magazines. "I thought we could do a working lunch. I've requested jam sandwiches to be served, and an excellent vintage of ginger-beer."

Peter sighed with satisfaction. "Absolutely ripping. Oh look, this one's got 'Metal Men from Mars'! Did they like the one with the model aeroplanes steered by wireless?"

"I believe they are giving it further study." While Peter was definitely the brains of the project, Sir Almsley served as the filter of realism for his wilder notions. A remotely piloted craft was too fantastic for even the Germans to fall for. In a similar vein, the trivial idea Peter had thought merely a good practical joke was presently causing no end of destruction in the paranoid Third Reich. Who would have thought a simple diagram of a dead rat stuffed with dynamite would cause so much panic? But there was never a shortage of real dead rats in a war zone and thanks to Peter's sketch the Germans thought every one could be a bomb and took steps accordingly. In Sir Almsley's considered opinion, Peter's practical joke had been every bit as effective as a bombing run.

"I did enjoy the plan for the secret zeppelin base in the Himalayas, however—brought back memories of my time in India. I fear the cost of construction will be prohibitive until the war is over, but I do hope they build it eventually. I should like to visit again."

"They should do a secret base on the Moon!" Peter grabbed one of the sandwiches and devoured it. "Bet the

Metal Men of Mars wouldn't expect that!"

"Indeed." Sir Almsley smiled at his co-conspirator. The numbing silence of his home was a thing of the past, and they had both found a way to help the war effort despite their limitations. Perhaps the two of them could one day make war a thing of the past as well. "Now, what else do we have to work with here?"

THE INSPECTION

Lieutenant Commander Gus Morton glared at the radioman hovering in the doorway of his cabin. Molumphy's usually expressive face was slack, and he had both hands raised in front of him as if he were holding a piece of paper—but his hands were empty. With an effort, Morton bottled his temper. Snapping at Molumphy would make him lose the image.

"Message for me?" he said in what he liked to think was a gentle tone.

"Um, yes, Cap'n." The vacant stare continued. God, he hated this. But how many sub captains had a radioman who could receive messages that hadn't been sent yet?

"Why don't you read it to me? My eyes are tired."

That worked. Molumphy looked down at the invisible sheet of typewritten message.

"USS *Fintan* report NSB New London for inspection and refit by 05-15-45"

Don't yell at Molumphy. Don't yell at Molumphy. Morton found himself gripping the edge of the tiny formica-covered desk so tightly the edges cut into his fingers. "Thanks, Molumphy. Carry on." Panic bubbled through him, first immobilizing and then launching him through the door where Molumphy had stood, whacking his head painfully on the low lintel. "Dammit!" Morton rubbed his forehead until the stars faded. "Saunders! Where the hell is Saunders? How can that giant hayseed hide in a sub, anyway?"

"XO's up top, Cap'n," a grimy Wogan volunteered. "Cook's girl's payin' us a visit."

Morton swallowed another corrosive burst of profanity, spun on his heel, and darted back into his cabin. The precious, flimsy wooden box in his kit had only one cigar left, and he hesitated before grabbing it. His last Cuban! But a deal was a deal, and she'd earned it. Plus, as the Germans had learned, it would be a bad idea to piss her off.

He stuffed the cigar in his front pocket to climb the

conning tower ladder. Flinging open the outer hatch, he tripped on the sill and nearly fell flat on the narrow deck. "SAUNDERS!" he screamed, in the general direction of the knot of crew gathered at the bow. "Do I have to fight the entire war by myself? And who authorized a party, you idiots? We've got work to do!"

Saunders slouched over, the sleepy grin on his face undiminished by Morton's accusations. "Just saying hello to Mitzi, Captain. What's the drill? Mitzi's people say the sea is clear for miles."

"Well that's one bit of good news. Which doesn't make up for the fact that we will be be ordered back to port in less than a month. *For inspection.*" Morton was gratified to see the grin on Saunders's face vanish. At least *someone* else grasped the danger.

"Molumphy got a future WARNO, sir?"

"Correct." Morton looked about the top surface of *Fintan*, hoping for inspiration. Unfortunately he caught sight of the symmetrical, curved pattern of indentations along the shield piece of the deck gun. It was quite clearly a bite mark from something with a three-foot-wide jaw and teeth that could leave holes in steel. "Gaah! How the hell are we going to explain *that?*"

"Storm damage", Saunders said, making a swinging

motion with an invisible hammer. "Just make it a little bit worse, nobody will notice."

"Some storm! And what about the rest of the ship? Those things had claws too. We need to check under the waterline." And if it hadn't been for Mitzi and her people, *Fintan* and crew would have been just another missing sub chalked up to the Nazis. Reminded of his duty, Morton made his way to the bow and the crowd of sailors still gathered there. Cookie was flat on the deck and apparently arm-wrestling Mitzi. She was winning.

Mitzi looked up as Morton approached and grinned. Morton tried hard not to shudder, but she *did* have an awful lot of sharp teeth. Whoever had written the legends of mermaids either had left some important details out, or hadn't met Mitzi's branch of the tribe. Her scaly section was more like an armored alligator than a fish, too, but from the look in Cookie's eyes he didn't see anything amiss in his girlfriend. To be fair, Cookie was no movie-star himself.

Morton touched the brim of his cap politely. "I am pleased to see you are none the worse from your exertions in the recent fight, ma'am," Morton said, reaching for the cigar in his pocket. "We couldn't ask for better allies. On behalf of myself and the crew of the

Fintan, please accept—"

Mitzi lunged, snagging the cigar in her mouth and diving over the side, slapping the water with her tail with a resounding splash. Morton checked his fingers for blood. He'd held the cigar by the very end for precisely that reason. Mitzi *loved* cigars, even though she ate them rather than smoked them. Something like catnip for mermaids.

"Got some bad news for you, Cookie. We're heading back soon. I'll need you to break the news to, uh, Miss Mitzi when she calms down."

"No prollem, Cap'n. Her 'n her people can follow, easy." At least that's what he thought Cookie said. He had some ungodly Southern accent combined with a twice-broken jaw which made him completely incomprehensible at times.

Morton's temper started to boil again. "That's what I'm afraid of, Cookie. What if somebody saw her? Official Naval policy is mermaids don't exist! We don't need them poking around to see what else they missed!"

He stomped off, yelling for Saunders to follow him. A sudden strong wind swung the hatch door into his face when he opened it and he swore. Back in his cabin he scrounged up a tablet of lined paper and a pencil.

Saunders followed shortly afterward, oozing his tall frame easily through the narrow door and avoiding the low lintel with an ease that never failed to irritate Morton. It wasn't fair. The man was taller, but it was always Morton that was hitting his head on things.

At his gesture, Saunders shut the door and sat on the bunk. "We've got plenty of time to hide the damage, Captain. What are you worried about?"

Morton glared at him. "I'm making a list. Ivek Siggurson, for one. Then Mitzi and her people. What if Fluffy follows us home? He's getting pretty big now and shows up nice and bright even on normal sonar. Then there's Molumphy and his crystal-ball brain, the fact that Wogan can now see in the dark, and, oh yes, we've expended eight torpedoes against kraken, a giant sea serpent, a phosphorescent pirate ship, and a horde of nameless scaly horrors of the deep but *not* German subs. And the crew took part in an actual boarding action, led by aformentioned authentic genuine Viking. I *am* looking forward to writing up my report. How about you? They'll set aside a whole wing in the mental hospital just for us!"

Saunders waved his hand. "Siggurson will do whatever you tell him to, Captain. According to Olsen he thinks you are a warrior sent by the gods or something. So we put him on an island and wave goodbye. Not like we can put him back on that sinking longboat, right?"

"I hate to abandon him," Morton grumbled. "He's a good fighter. Berserked that first time he experienced depth charges, but sound man, sound. But he's not on the crew list. What about the rest?"

"Molumphy—we'll give him some morphine and say he's got, oh, I don't know, recurring laryngitis? They won't keep us in port forever, war's still on last time I looked. I'll remind Wogan to keep quiet. As for the rest," he shrugged. "You've been keeping a second log ever since the storm. We just need to come up with a better version for the log you hand in. It's not like we didn't sink plenty of Germans."

"Fluffy got most of them, but I take your point. I just hope nobody intercepted that one ship's Mayday call."

Saunders grinned. "You mean the one where he was yelling 'Mein Gott, the eyes, the eyes!'? Yeah, that might be awkward. We'll just say he was drunk."

Morton grunted. It might work. "We'll have to make sure the crew knows the official story too. It won't do to have another version floating around. And what about Fluffy? Poor little guy. After we killed his mother it just doesn't seem right to put him in danger."

"He thinks *Fintan* is his mother now, but he's getting big enough he'll be heading out on his own soon. He's a *kraken*, for heaven's sake. We're not feeding him enough." Saunders cocked his head. "That's not what has your tail in a knot, Captain. What's the real problem?"

Morton sat silently for a moment, staring at the bulkhead. He felt cold. "I'm worried about *Fintan*," he said finally. "If they ever find out what she can do, they'll take her apart, down to the last rivet. Just to find out what makes her tick. After all she's done for us, how can I let that happen?"

Saunders looked dubious. "She's a good sub, sir, but what's so special that would get noticed?"

"Haven't you noticed what happened after the storm, right after the lightning hit us? Sure, Molumphy had his little foggy moments before that but he never got radio messages from the future. I swear the radio changed to pick things up that only he can hear. Same thing with Fluffy. First off, remember how the engines died and wouldn't restart? Just when the mother kraken was nearby and we hadn't figured out the sonar profile? And then when she was dead the hull made the same kind of noises she had, and Fluffy didn't attack, just snuggled up and hung on to the tower. And the the time we rocked hard, with the sea smooth as glass, and Cookie fell overboard right near Mitzi's lagoon? The sonar alone would be bad enough. It's so accurate you can practically see the serial number on the enemy propellers!"

"Yeah, the sonar. You're right, they'd notice that. And how quiet the engines have gotten. The Germans can't pick us up at all. OK, what's our story?"

For the next two weeks Morton rarely left his cabin except to inspect the "repair" crew's efforts. Between him and Saunders they had cobbled together a sequence of events that covered all the damage they couldn't cover up, the torpedoes expended, known German ships sunk, and the few encounters with other US submarines. Then, fueled by some of Cookie's extra-thick coffee, Morton laboriously copied the details into the official log. He diluted the ink in his pen progressively so the text wouldn't look so uniform, and even wrapped his fingers to make his handwriting shakier for a few entries ("depth charge attack sustained, minor injury").

They'd found a nice island off the main trade routes for Siggurson. Olson, the only one who understood even a little of what the time-traveling castaway said, confided Siggurson thought he was being left behind because he wasn't good enough to go to Valhalla with them. The Viking had looked quite doleful until Morton, wracked with guilt, gave him his own hat. ("Service cover washed overboard in storm").

By then the real radio message had been received. Cookie made a big pile of rancid Spam, Fluffy's favorite treat, and they fired it out the Number Two torpedo tube at maximum pressure. A lump in his throat, Morton watched the baby kraken swim happily after it, and ordered the ship rigged for silent running, maximum speed. Mitzi had said she'd keep an eye on him. Morton hoped he'd be OK, and wouldn't forget how to distinguish US subs from German ones.

Meanwhile, the officers had been drilling the crew on their stories. Morton kept hearing the conversations and his nervousness increased.

"No, Gruner, we went over that. You got your injury when the torpedo slipped in the rack. *We never boarded any ships*, got that? And you didn't follow any Viking up a rope."

"Mewhinney, you did not train Fluffy to attack anyone speaking German. Fluffy doesn't exist. Review your battle cards again, OK? Fluffy NEVER HAPPENED."

When *Fintan* was only half an hour out from the slips, Molumphy reported for his morphine shot. The pages of the real log book had been carefully hidden in a false bottom of Morton's trunk and the rest of the sub carefully sanitized. They'd tried to deliberately de-tune the sonar, but it kept drifting back to the fine detail setting. Morton shrugged, resigned. He'd just have to hope nobody turned it on while the sub was docked.

Then he had to go ashore. The first part of the review board was routine, and he started to relax. He'd spent so much time memorizing the fake story it all flowed naturally.

"So, how was it you spent nearly a year without coming back to base?"

Ooops. "We wanted to stay in the fight, sir. Why waste time in transit when we could be supplied at sea?" That had taken some effort, and a few of Molumphy's future intercepts, to pull off. Especially getting provisioned only at night. He *really* didn't want to remember loading the torpedoes by hand either, but it had gotten done.

"You had some unusual requisitions, too. A whole *crate* of Spam?"

Beads of sweat formed on his forehead. "My crew enjoyed it, sir. I felt morale was improved." *My crew that had tentacles certainly enjoyed it...* Morton heard mutters about "only sub in the fleet that can say that," but no further questions followed on that topic.

"I did not see any notation about training and advancement work. While the war is going well, you really must think about your crew and continuous improvement. The Hun will fight to the end! But I see that you have done fairly well for yourself," the senior officer said, shuffling papers and looking sour. "The Germans appear to be avoiding your sector now. In fact, a report has surfaced one U-boat captain refused to patrol there and was shot by the SS. I don't place much reliance on it, since it claims he cited 'monsters' as the reason. Someone in Washington believed you're behind it, since you have been put in for some medals. I suppose the paperwork will be along soon."

"Thank you, sir," Morton said, stunned. "I...I must say, none of it would have been possible without the superior abilities and courage of my crew." *And my sub.*

And Siggurson. And Mitzi. And Fluffy. He lifted his chin. "It was my honor to serve with them."

It was late when they finished with him, and he walked out of the building into the cool night air. Morton found himself walking along the dock where *Fintan* was tied up, looking just like any other *Turbot*-class submarine. He nodded to the sentry, saying "Just want to give her one last check." When out of sight, he laid a hand on the conning tower. "I think we fooled them, old girl. You're safe." The relief he felt was profound. Now he was tired, and all he wanted was a large drink at the O-club and a bed that didn't have bulkheads on either end.

The sentry saluted as he growled, "Keep a good watch on her, she's been through a lot," and walked away. He thought he knew the shortcut to the O-club, but the warehouses all looked the same in the dark and he soon realized he was in the wrong area. Then he saw car headlights, and quickened his step. He could ask for directions.

But when he got close enough to ask, the shadowy figures weren't wearing uniforms. "This area is closed to civilians," Morton started to say, but two of the men just picked him up by the arms and carried him off.

A warehouse door was opened by one of the shadowy men. The warehouse was full to the rafters with mysterious wooden crates, all unlabeled. "Dammit, wrong door. Sorry, bud," the man said to a fellow in dungaree coveralls, pushing a crate with scorchmarks on the side.

Morton struggled but to no avail. "What the hell do you think you are doing? Who are you people? Saboteurs? You'll never get away with it, and I won't tell you anything!"

The next door they tried showed an empty space, except for three people—one, strangely, a woman who looked exactly like a middle-aged office secretary, down to the purse and glasses on a chain about her neck. She was holding a clipboard, and looking at him over the glasses with a faintly disapproving expression. The iron grip on Morton's arms released, and he looked back. Two burly men in trenchcoats and hard expressions were between him and the door.

"What's going on here?" Morton snapped.

One of the men standing in the center of the room spoke. "Lieutenant Commander Morton. We want to talk to you about your recent activities. The *true* version, if you please."

Panic spiked. The review board must have figured it out. He hadn't fooled them after all. "I already told the board everything. If you don't believe me, check my log. Besides, how do I know you aren't Germans?"

The man sighed. "This is a bit irregular, I agree, but we are not German spies. Secrecy, however, required our somewhat forceful invitation. Allow me to show my identification." The papers he presented looked official enough, and they weren't in German.

Morton glared at the man suspiciously. Not the review board. But how had they known? Why were they here? "What do you want from me?"

"We want to offer you a job."

"I'm not at liberty to accept. As a Naval Officer, during wartime—"

"Yes, well, you may have started another one. Not your fault, really, but I suppose you didn't notice the mark on the side of that kraken you took out, did you? Now Atlantis thinks we're attacking them and we really can't have that spill over into the *other* war." The man leaned closer. "We need you, Morton. You, and your crew, and your submarine. *Especially* your submarine."

Morton gulped. They knew about *Fintan*. "Who's 'we'?"

The man smiled. "The Bureau of Substandards. And you and your crew will fit in rather well."

Author's note: The crew names in this story were obtained from actual WWII sub captains. Yes, they are strange.

A DAY SPENT FISHING

The first time Ruyken saw his death, he didn't recognize it. Even though death was in his thoughts at the time, leaving the doctor's office with the heavy confirmation numbing his mind. A swirl of wind gusted up from the ground carrying a feather, a scrap of paper, and a dry leaf. Nothing unusual.

As he worked in his garden, he saw it again without knowing. Dust circled on a path before him as he carried his tools back to the shed in a wheelbarrow, but he was thinking of the seeds he'd collected last fall, and whether the Shasta daisies would do well in the meadow. Anything was better than thinking of the weight that dragged in his chest, the weight that would someday bring him down.

The swirling grew larger as the weeks passed, and carried more with it. A handful of straw, fragments of leaf mold, a pale blue shard of bird's egg. He stared at it one summer day, dusting his hands on his faded overalls and remembering the tornadoes he'd seen all too many times on his farm. When he still had the farm. But that was in the Midwest, where the weather was as large as the land. Now he was old and lived in a gentler place, where tornadoes did not venture.

Ruyken commented on it one day to his neighbor. "It happens on hot days sometimes," the man said, shrugging.

"But so often?" Ruyken wondered, pointing at the twist of dust that hung over the gravel road before them.

His neighbor looked at him, puzzled, then at where he was pointing. "Must've died down. They don't last long, you know."

Ruyken nodded slowly, feeling cold. The swirling dust was still there.

He asked others, cautiously. Only he could see it. Now that he knew he could see it was always with him. In the house it picked up dust motes and dried flower petals fallen from a vase. In the doctor's office papers rustled on the desk as he waited.

As the days passed it grew stronger. Its strength increased as his diminished, with each examination that confirmed his heart was wearing out. He'd had a hard life, taking work that broke his health to feed his family. After he'd lost the farm what else could he do?

He understood it now; understood why he alone could see it. It was his death. A constant reminder that followed him, robbing his last days of pleasure.

It hovered beside him as he turned the compost. "Leave me alone," he whispered, clutching his pitchfork tightly, wishing he could strike at it like the rats that came to steal cabbage stalks. The death ignored him.

Sometimes he could forget. Lost in the simple, mechanical action of weeding, feeling the summer sun loosen the stiffness of his hands, seeing only the rich soil and the golden dust of pollen on bright petals. And one day breathing in the thick air of his greenhouse, full of the scent of flowers and moist earth, his granddaughter watching with wide, fascinated eyes as he used his old brass mister on the orchids. He casually set it on a bench, low enough for her four-year-old hands to reach, and smiled inside when she was unable to resist the temptation.

But then he saw the death outside through the dusty

windows, and a surge of bitterness ran through him. He wanted to see his orchids bloom. He wanted to see his granddaughter grow up. The death was so strong now, almost as tall and broad as he was. He knew his time was short. Every day, every hour, it came closer to him.

The next day they went fishing. The days were getting shorter now, and the morning air crisp. His granddaughter looked even smaller sitting in the big, old-fashioned car, a fishing rod twice as tall as she was clutched in her hands. They were early, and no-one else was at the river dock. His death followed him only a foot behind.

His granddaughter ran out on the dock and he called to her to wait, his concern erasing all his other worries. But she slowed down of her own accord at the dock edge, one arm clutching a piling as she gazed doubtfully down at the clear water.

Rukyen brought the bait and the plastic pail for their catches. His granddaughter watched with thoughtful solemnity as he baited her hook, and showed her how to hold the rod.

It was a beautiful day; the sun bright and a light breeze off the river that carried the sound of bullfrogs from the marshy area nearby, and a solitary red-winged blackbird. Swallows swooped and skimmed over the surface of the water. The river was clear and slightly golden, and he could see the fish begin to drift closer and flick away. He sighed, content, then looked around, remembering.

His death was not there. Always it followed him, like a dog. But here he was, at the end of the dock, and nothing disturbed the cast of sand by his feet or the milkweed fluff that had gathered in the lee of a piling.

Was he free?

He propped his rod in a handy knothole in the dock decking, and walked back to the car for their lunch. As soon as he stepped off the dock a single skeletal leaf spiraled up from the ground, floating at eye level, soon joined by a maple wing and a scattering of rusty pine needles. He snatched the lunch basket from the seat and hurried back, glancing behind him. The dust and leaves subsided to the ground as soon as he stepped on the dock.

So. It would not follow him here. He felt shaky with emotion, unsure of the meaning. He picked up his rod again, breathing deeply. A few moments later, he felt the gentle tug of bait being taken. He pulled with equal gentleness, setting the hook before the fish could realize the danger.

He looked over at his granddaughter. She had pulled up her line with one hand, carefully examining the bait still on the hook as if she might have overlooked a fish. He smiled. She was very patient for her age, but he could see her frustration.

"Oh, goodness. Look what I've done. We've gotten the fishing rods mixed up. See? I have yours. No wonder it isn't working." The exchange made, he waited with glee until she pulled up her line once again. Her eyes were as big as saucers when she saw the rainbow trout on the other end. He helped her bring it in, quickly removing the hook and stunning the fish against the piling so the flapping would not distress her.

She didn't catch any more fish, but she didn't seem to mind. He caught two more before looking at his watch and realizing the hour with horror. He'd completely forgotten the time–and he had so little left.

What was he going to do? He had to take his granddaughter home. He had forgotten the death when it was not before him, reminding him, and now he might only have a few seconds, a few minutes–he had no way to know.

His granddaughter was kneeling on the dock, both

hands on the edge of the pail as she studied the fish inside. He wondered if she understood what had happened to them.

"What are we going to do with the fishes?" she wanted to know.

"Have them for dinner," Rukyen answered, hoping he would.

She looked at him, solemnly, and then back at the fish. She reached in and touched one carefully, as if she were afraid she would wake it.

He let her carry the pail back to the car. He hesitated at the edge of the dock, then lifted his chin and stepped on the bank. The death rose up before him, but he kept walking straight at it, determined to hold it back for just a little longer. It was so strong he could no longer see through it. Death was always strong. It had to be. Life came from death, as any gardener knew. He would die, but first he would take his granddaughter home.

When he was almost touching his death it moved away. Rukyen halted, puzzled. It was the same distance from him as it had been that morning. Almost a whole day, and nothing had changed? A fragment of memory, a proverb, teased at him. Something about the hours spent fishing being counted in a different way.

Confused, fragmented thoughts flashed through his mind, holding him immobile. Maybe he could live forever, if he stayed on the dock. He didn't want to live forever on the dock, exiled from his garden. His granddaughter would get cold and frightened before anyone found them. It would be a shame to waste the fish.

Slowly his mind calmed. Nothing had really changed. He had been granted a brief forgetfulness, and an option that offered life but nothing that he wanted to live for. He still had a little time. Certainly enough time to have dinner, and one last evening in his garden. He really should make sure the roses were watered before he left.

Rukyen walked to the car and opened the door. On the seat was the old paper sack he always took with him. It was soft with use, and inside were seeds he'd saved; poppies, cosmos, bachelor button, love-in-the-mist, and other favorites from his garden. When he drove by any place roadwork had torn the ground he would reach in and toss seeds out the window, knowing the next year the ugly roadside would be covered with color.

He took the sack and walked back to the dock,

where the bank was bare from erosion. Flinging handfuls of seeds one after the other he emptied the sack, the lighter seeds carried by the breeze from the river. Some even swirled for a moment in the death that stood beside him.

Folding the paper sack carefully, he walked back to the car. His granddaughter was holding the pail of fish on her lap as if it were something rare and precious.

Rukyen smiled at her. "There. Now I'm ready to go."

THE CORRECT WAY TO FILL OUT FORM PCR-103-U

<u>Section 3.a Describe Precipitating Event</u>

Boris Niels dabbed at an incipient drop of sweat and looked around, hoping he would see something familiar. The ancient linoleum squares were exactly the same depressing color as they were in the hallway outside his office and grimy with dust in the same way, but it was not his hallway. He wasn't even sure it was the same building. All of the doors were wood, thickly coated with multiple layers of government-issued paint, and labeled with a sequence of numbers and letters that would presumably thwart any spies that penetrated the outer defenses of the Bureau of Divisional Substandards and Measures in search of a particular location. They had certainly thwarted Niels.

It's only my third day on the job, he though morosely, and wiped his forehead again. Somehow the building air conditioning was able to cool the interior while simultaneously retaining all the humidity, which was a violation of Boyle's law and a few zoning ordinances. *I can't afford to be lost. What will Director Bunsford say?*

Director Bunsford had hired him, even though Niels could see no reason for the Bureau of Divisional Substandards and Measures having any use for an easily-distracted forensic accountant. He'd even worked up the courage to say as much, but Bunsford had dismissed his concerns with a swirling sea of sonorous, half-muffled and incomplete phrases about potential and resourcefulness. Niels felt like he was being submerged in marshmallow. Director Bunsford gave the impression of marshmallow in his appearance as well, as if it featured in some distant branch of his family tree.

He'd also mumbled something about "seeing where you fit in first" when Niels had asked about his duties. So, Niels had spent his time reading the binder full of Department rules and procedures that had been issued to him by the fearsomely efficient Miss Adenaur. He'd even had to sign for it, and he felt a little frisson of excitement when he saw the official government header and warnings against removing it from the building or communicating its contents to any individual not cleared to receive its secrets.

The excitement swiftly waned in the days that followed. Niels sat in his bare, dusty office on a hard wooden chair, in front of a massive metal desk that looked like it had a secondary function as a bomb shelter, and tried to work his way through the binder. At noon he ate his sandwich, still at his desk, and tried to read more. The dust was bothering him, and with a spurt of adventure he decided to look for a vending machine. It was after all, he reasoned, an office building even if it was a government office building and office buildings had vending machines. With cold drinks in them. Maybe even a grape soda. Niels was very fond of grape soda, a fondness not shared by whoever usually stocked vending machines.

He had wandered up stairs and through hallways, now thoroughly lost but he had decided, with a shrug, if he was lost he might as well stay lost until he found a vending machine. Then he would be lost with a drink. A cold, richly grape-flavored drink. He could almost taste it. And why hadn't he seen anyone else? The doors were closed and he didn't dare knock and disturb anyone, but surely there would be other people working in the department and walking about? Now that he thought about it, in the three days he'd worked here the only people he'd seen were Director Bunsford, Miss Adenaur, and a janitor mopping the hallway.

A barely audible humming noise alerted him, the distinctive sound of a mechanical apparatus possibly employed in cooling drinks. Niels rounded the corner of yet another identical hallway, and there it was. An ancient vending machine, the kind that dispensed glass bottles from a rack with wire clamps holding the bottles like the business end of a mousetrap. The glass door was dusty, but Niels could see the bottles and a feebly flickering red light next to the "No Change" sign. Well, he always carried enough coins to make change for any value so that should be no problem. He drew a breath. One of the bottle caps was purple. Could it be?

He fed in the requested 35 cents, marveling that the price was old-fashioned too. They were charging a dollar and a half at the airports and they didn't have grape soda in glass bottles. The bottle, once he wrestled it free from the wire trap, was icy cold. Niels popped the metal cap off with the opener fastened to the side of the vending machine, and out of habit, checked the coin return slot. There was a coin in it.

Even cheaper than 35 cents! rejoiced Niels, and he held up the coin to see how much he had saved. It was hexagonal, a soft, frosted-gold color, and he couldn't read the writing or recognize any of the symbols on it. It wasn't American. He wasn't even sure it was human.

Section 3.b List All Incidents Observed and Actions Taken (use additional paper if needed)

By the time Niels found his way back to familiar ground he had drunk all the grape soda and was thirsty again. The janitor was still mopping the hallway, and Niels frowned, looking at his watch. He'd been gone nearly an hour and the guy was still mopping the same bit of floor? He glanced out of the corner of his eye. The janitor was hunched over, had hairy eyebrows that blended seamlessly with his shaggy hair and scruffy beard, and wore a coverall with what looked like oil stains scattered over most of the surface. Niels shrugged. Maybe it just took him that long to mop.

The strange coin weighed heavily in his pocket. Maybe it was gold. Maybe it was an archaeological artifact, put in by mistake by an absent-minded professor. Who just happened to visit the Bureau of Substandards on his way to report on his findings from an ancient Mayan tomb. Niels sighed, and decided to seek help.

Miss Adenaur was typing, on an actual typewriter, a prim and somewhat disapproving expression on her narrow face. Her grey hair was pulled back in a tight bun that was probably bullet-proof. The sweater around her shoulders was precisely arranged and fastened by the top button, leaving her arms free, and she had her half-glasses perched on her nose with a chain of faded plastic beads dangling from them and around her neck. Her resemblance to his third-grade teacher was uncanny.

When Niels approached her desk, she looked up and gave him an impatient glance over her glasses. "If you need to see Director Bunsford he is away at an off-site meeting and won't be back until tomorrow," she said.

"Er, no. That is, I was hoping you could advise me on what I should do with this," he said, and showed her the odd coin. "I found it, and it looks like it might be valuable."

To Niels' great surprise, Miss Adenaur stopped typing and stared at the coin, then at him. She looked shocked. "Where did you find that?" she snapped.

"It was in the coin return of the vending machine upstairs," Niels said, blinking. That had not been the reaction he was expecting.

"Nonsense. We don't have vending machines in this building." Niels held up the empty grape soda bottle. Condensation was still visible on the outside of the bottle, and a small dribble of purple liquid was rolling around inside. Miss Adenaur took the bottle gingerly, and inspected it through her half-glasses. Now she looked worried. "I think you had better show me this vending machine. I wish the Director was here," she muttered, removing the paper she had been typing with a zip of the roller and closing it in a safe marked "Classified". She took a large, crowded ring of keys from her desk drawer and placed them in a white purse with metal corners. She shooed Niels out of the office and locked it behind her. "All right, where is it?"

Not knowing what else to do, Niels went back down the hallway, attempting to recreate his path. As they walked past the still-mopping janitor, Miss Adenaur said irritably, "I don't know how there could be any unexpected vending machines in this building. We don't get any deliveries for them either. If someone has installed one without the Director's permission we need to find out who did it." The janitor looked up at her through shaggy brows, and then returned to his mopping.

Niels went up stairs and down hallways, not seeing the vending machine and painfully aware of the growing expression of skepticism on Miss Adenaur's pinched face. All he had wanted was a grape soda. He could use another one now, with all this stair climbing and walking. Cool, refreshing, rich grape soda …

He turned the corner, and there it was. Still humming away contentedly, with frost on the glass door coyly hiding the bottles inside.

Miss Adenaur gasped, and strode indignantly to the machine. "How *dare* they!" she said, her voice quivering. "It's very old. I haven't seen one like that for years. I didn't know they were still in use," she added thoughtfully. She placed her half-glasses firmly on her nose and gave the vending machine a close inspection. "The Director should know about this," she said slowly, as if she was worried.

"It's just a vending machine," Niels said. "Why is it a problem?" There was still a grape soda inside, and he fed more coins in. "Would you like something, Miss Adenaur?" He pulled out his grape soda and set it on top of the machine.

"Does it have anything diet?" she asked dubiously. "Oh, there. That one, please." The top was a shocking pink. Niels pulled it out and handed it to her, noticing as he did so the "No Change" light had gone out.

Miss Adenaur took a careful sip. "It certainly *tastes* like soda," she conceded.

Niels suddenly had an idea. The strange coin had gone through the machine because it couldn't make change. But now it should work. "I wonder what this will do?" he said, and took out the gold coin.

"NO!" shrieked Miss Adenaur, but it was too late. The mysterious coin made a solid chunking noise as it descended through the vending machine—and then everything stopped being normal. The machine stretched and expanded like taffy, multicolored lightning spreading over it and through the air like very expensive special effects. Niels felt as if he were being turned inside out, and then back again. *This is much better than a 3-D movie.*

Then suddenly it stopped. The dingy government-issued hallway had vanished, replaced by a rocky cavern lit by giant wrought-iron torches with lots of spikes coming out of them. Niels and Miss Adenaur were standing on a circular stone platform inscribed with strange symbols very similar to the ones he remembered on the gold coin.

Standing around the stone platform were several scaly, monstrous individuals with horned helmets and armor and swords and.... Niels blinked. Several scaly, monstrous <u>horned</u> individuals. "Ooops." he said.

The creatures moved forward, gripping their weapons and grinning in an unfriendly way. Miss Adenaur screamed and threw her diet soda at them. Immediately the monsters howled in agony, slapping where the soda had splashed them and crashing into each other trying to get away. Niels saw a tunnel off to one side and grabbed Miss Adenaur's arm. "Run!"

They ran until Niels had a stitch in his side and was gasping for air. All he wanted was someplace to hide. Every time they saw one of the creatures he'd dodge down a side tunnel until they were hopelessly lost. The tunnels were damp and moisture dripped from above. Niels stepped on something strange and squishy that gleeped and then went silent.

"In there!" whispered Miss Adenaur, pointing to an opening in the tunnel wall. Cobwebs draped the edges of the opening, and when Niels took a cautious look the small room appeared unoccupied.

"What was...who...where *are* we?" moaned Niels. He sat down on a dusty, iron-bound chest. "Am I really seeing these things? Or was the grape soda past its sell-by date?" He grimaced, recalling his second soda was still on top of the vending machine—assuming the vending machine hadn't eaten it when it morphed. He could use a grape soda now.

Miss Adenaur was gasping for air too, but she did not seem too distressed. Niels stared at her. A trickle of grey was running down her face, and a splotch of hair now showed a different color. A light gold color.

"You dye your hair?" he said incredulously.

Miss Adenaur glared at him. "What a rude thing to say! I certainly do not <u>dye</u> my hair. I merely...color it."

"You color it. Grey. Why?"

She sniffed. "Bureau of Substandards dress code for administrative assistants, Mr. Niels. We strive to keep a certain appearance at all times. I'm not really a full admin, I'm just filling in for Miss Gruntheiss while she's on vacation. She thought I looked too young for such a position of responsibility, so she suggested the hair color. I suppose I should have spent the extra to get the waterproof version." She shivered, and put her arms through the dangling sleeves of her sweater. "I don't think we are in the Bureau building any more, do you?"

"Well, the tunnels are certainly not ADA-compliant," Niels said. "And I think the Fire Marshal would have multiple seizures about the torches everywhere. So, no."

"Is that what you were thinking about while running and dodging those...things?" Miss Adenaur said, admiringly.

"I have a tendency to get distracted under stress," Niels admitted. "That's what lost me my last job." He peered out the doorway. Shadows moved in the distance, and he drew back.

"And what was your previous job, Mr. Niels?" Miss Adenaur dusted a corner of the chest with her handkerchief and sat down.

"Forensic Accountant with the DA's office, organized crime division."

"Oooh, how exciting! Gangsters! Did you catch any?"

Niels winced. "Not exactly. Well, it didn't go to trial."

"Why not?"

"He blew up. I *know* I told them about the

fireworks, it showed up in the cash flow documentation. He was buying just enough each time to avoid triggering the explosives mandatory reporting—which would have also triggered the storage permit audit—and I pointed this out but they were looking for tax dodges. So when they went to arrest him, he hid down in the bunker with all the fireworks and a stray bullet set it all off."

"Well, at least he got what was coming to him," Miss Adenaur said.

"Unfortunately the explosion destroyed most of the evidence and his family sued for reckless endangerment and felony littering. The DA's office fired me before the investigation found out I was on record as warning about the fireworks." Niels sighed. Somehow, no matter how he tried, it never went right. Just look where a simple grape soda had gotten him. He glanced out the doorway again. This time there was no sign of any activity. "We'd better find a way back to the Bureau."

All the tunnels looked alike so they wound up following groups of the armed scaly creatures at a careful distance. It took several nerve-wracking hours, with the only sustenance some mints Miss Adenaur had in her purse. Unfortunately, when they found the large cavern they had first been transported to there weren't many places to hide in it. The only place of concealment was a huge, ugly statue behind the stone platform Niels had not noticed earlier, mostly because he was running away screaming in the opposite direction at the time.

"There's too much light," he whispered to Miss Adenaur. "We might be able to sneak by some of the guards if it was just a little darker." She nodded. Niels looked around for inspiration. The clammy tunnel walls had odd rubbery lichens and other things growing on them, and the floors grew transparent blobs that looked like mushrooms. He stepped on one, and it gleeped with a squish. He tried pulling one of the lichens away, but was unable to get any loose until Miss Adenaur took out a metal nail file from her purse. The lichen shrank away from the metal as if it were burned.

Niels gathered a handful of lichen strands and knotted them together in a loose rope. Then he pulled up a handful of the blobs. He grabbed both ends of the lichen rope, pulled it back with a blob in place, and let fly.

His first attempt missed. The second did too, but much closer to the torch he was aiming for. Luckily the guard-creatures were making so much noise grunting and banging their weapons they did not notice the faint gleeping and squishing.

He hit the first torch. It struggled to stay alight for a moment, then gave up in a puff of green smoke. Another miss, then the second torch went out.

"Oh, good shot!" said Miss Adenaur. A patch of gloom covered their side of the cavern. Niels waited until the guard-creatures were involved in some intense discussion before running low for the back of the statue, pulling Miss Adenaur behind him. "Now what do we do?"

Niels placed a handful of blobs on a handy outcrop of the statue, just in case. "There must be a way to use that platform to get back. How else would they be able to get to our world and leave that coin behind?"

"I suppose so," Miss Adenaur said doubtfully. "But when—"

Suddenly the statue they were leaning against started to shake. Glancing out from the side, Niels saw a few puffs of orange smoke and what looked like sparklers. Compared to the amazing lightning of the vending machine, this was hardly impressive. The guard-creatures, however, reacted with wails and dropped to their knees, bowing down with scaly arms outstretched. From somewhere inside the statue two beings emerged. They were also scaly, but in a more elegant, snakelike way and wore flowing robes.

"It issss time," one said. "The humanssss sssuspect nothing."

"Yesss," said the other. "We ssshall take the Key and all dimensssssionss will be oursss!"

The first held up a claw. "Firssst we musst find it. They hide it well. Ssssumon the troopsss!"

As the scaly armored creatures began to fill the cavern, Miss Adenaur tugged on Niels' sleeve. "We have to stop them!" she whispered frantically.

"What were they talking about? Do you know what key they want?"

"Yes! And they can't be allowed to have it!"

Niels carefully looked around the statue. A select group of the guard-creatures stood on the stone platform with the two slender snake-people. One of the snake people took a staff and whacked the statue on the right knee. The statue's leg kicked out, and as it moved a rippling disturbance of reality followed with the familiar rainbow-colored lightning threading through it all, engulfing the figures on the platform.

He glanced back at Miss Adenaur. She lifted her large, metal-edged purse with a grim smile. Niels gathered his handful of blobs, readied his slingshot, and jumped up on the now-empty platform. Miss Adenaur followed close behind. From the corner of his eye he saw her swing her purse with a mighty blow as he fired the squishy blobs at the surprised guards, and then the special effects started in. They had done it!

Section 3.c Resolution of Precipitating Event

Back in the real world Miss Adenaur sped away, Niels desperately trying to keep up. In moments they were back in their familiar hallway, complete with the familiar mopping janitor.

"Joe! Joe!" shrieked Miss Adenaur. "We have a foothold situation. Code 9!"

The shaggy, stooped figure stopped mopping and stood straight. Intelligent grey eyes coolly scanned the corridor, and with a single fluid motion Joe flung the yellow plastic "Danger Wet Surface" sign behind them. Niels heard a *whaaauuumm* noise and turned. The yellow plastic sign was creating a shimmering force field, blocking the corridor.

"Orders, Ma'am?"

Miss Adenaur rooted in her purse, pulling out the fat ring of keys. "I'm going to use the Form, Joe. Hold them off as long as you can."

"Yes Ma'am!" Joe grinned, revealing even white teeth behind the scruffy beard, and rolled up the oil-stained sleeves of his overalls. His forearms were heavily muscled. "I'm on the job."

Miss Adenaur was inserting one of the keys into a door marked "Maintenance". She turned it to the left, waited while counting under her breath, then turned it sharply to the right. "Come on!" she snapped, and jerked her head at the open door. The outside of the door was the usual painted wood, but the inside surface looked like the kind of thing you would see in a bank vault.

"But those creatures—we can't just leave one man to fight them all!" Niels protested.

"Joe is a highly trained Bureau security specialist," Miss Adenaur said. "We don't have much time, and I need you to authorize the Form or it will all be for nothing!"

She grabbed his wrist in an extremely firm grasp and hauled. Niels glanced back, struggling, and saw the janitor's cart had transformed itself into a robot with red glowing eyes and mechanical spider legs, that the brooms and mops had been unscrewed to reveal wicked blades inside, and Joe standing like an old West gunfighter, a squirt-bottle in each hand, guarding the doorway as the door closed slowly behind him.

"What's in those squirt-bottles?" he gasped as they ran. This corridor was gleaming and modern, multiple sensors and devices scanning them with red laser beams. Miss Adenaur was too busy yelling passwords to reply.

At the end of the corridor was another door, this one with a big steel wheel and heavy metal rods along the surface. There was also a head-shaped depression in the center. Miss Adenaur put her head inside. The door clicked, clanged, and slowly opened. Miss Adenaur shuffled backwards, her head still in the depression."Yu hff tu gu tru fst", she said, her voice muffled. "Gu!"

Niels hesitated. Miss Adenaur kicked him in the shins. Half-expecting to be shot with a death ray, he stepped inside the darkness and promptly tripped down a short flight of stairs.

The lights blinked on. "Sorry about that, but the door scanner wouldn't recognize you yet," Miss Adenaur said at the top of the stairs. The door slammed shut behind her and she ran down the stairs. Niels got painfully to his feet, and stared. Inside the room was a building. It looked like several of the small buildings scattered around the grounds of the Department, a single-story clapboard structure of WWII vintage. It had a roof, and windows. There was even the 55-gallon metal trash can out front.

"Wa...why?"

Miss Adenaur was using another key on her keyring to open the door. "I don't have time to explain. Listen! When you go inside sit down immediately at the desk. Don't touch anything except the chair, the desk, and the pen. This is important!"

There wasn't much else in the building. There was a door identical to the one they had just entered straight ahead. The desk and chair were on the left side of the room. On the right was a single three-drawer black metal filing cabinet, battered and scratched. On the side were faded yellow stenciled numbers. Miss Adenaur selected another key from the key ring, took a deep breath, and slowly approached the filing cabinet with the key outstretched in front of her as far as she could put it. She unlocked the filing cabinet with great care and opened the middle drawer, taking out a folder that gleamed faintly silver.

Niels sat down at the desk. There was a chipped plastic pen before him, and he picked it up. It warmed briefly and then went cool again.

"I need that," Miss Adenaur said, and took the pen from him. She opened one of the desk drawers and took out an index card box. It was full of the little sticky tape flags that said things like "Please Initial" and "Sign Here". Carefully lifting the form from the folder, she started filling in lines and affixing the "Sign Here" flags.

Niels heard a muffled boom and yelling coming from the corridor. "Um, I don't think we have time for this," he said. "We should go." He looked at the unopened door, estimating the distance. Would there be another exit from the big room, or was it just a closet?

"We have to do this right or it won't work," Miss Adenaur said through clenched teeth. Something slammed into the big steel door, making it bulge. Niels lunged for the door, only to be brought up short by Miss Adenaur's firm grasp of his collar. "Sit and sign!"

Niels sat. "How can I possibly sign for anything? I've only been here three days and I don't even have an assignment yet!" The form had at least ten pages, and he had to watch carefully to make sure he didn't sign where he was supposed to initial and vice versa. As he turned the pages the paper began to change, feeling cool and smooth like marble, yet the pen dragged as if it were being pulled in by a magnet. On the last page he had to use both hands, struggling and sweating to make the pen move.

"Hurry*! Hurry!* They've broken through the door!" Miss Adenaur shrieked.

With a supreme effort of will, feet braced against the wall, Niels pushed the pen through the final "s". *I am so glad I don't have a name like Hasendorferschein,* he thought, collapsing across the desk.

At first, nothing happened. Then the writing on the page began to glow, then shine, and finally the light was so bright Niels covered his eyes and scrabbled to hide under the desk. Horrible shrieking noises from the scaly other-dimensional creatures outside told him something was finally going right today.

Then the light abated and he crawled out from under the desk. Miss Adenaur was in the corner with her sweater over her head. "I think it's over," Niels said, sounding shaky. He looked outside. The dimensional creatures had melted into a pile of disgusting goo.

"It worked. It really worked," Miss Adenaur said softly, staggering a little. Niels held out his arm. Using each other for balance they picked their way across the floor and past the crumpled steel door. More piles of goo covered the hallway floor. Niels braced himself for what he might see outside.

Joe the Security Janitor was sitting against the wall, one eye swollen shut and completely covered in other-dimensional goo. He smiled. "Good job, kid. Lure 'em out and then smack 'em hard. They won't be back for a long time, not this bunch."

"Joe! You're alive!" said Niels, astonished.

Joe sneered. "Take more'n that to do for me, kid. All part of a day's work. And I was almost done mopping that section, too. Sneaky bastards. First time they tried a vending machine."

"What has been happening here?" The rich, sonorous tones of Director Bunsford's voice filled the hall, shortly followed by Director Bunsford filling the hall. If anything, he had gotten more marshmallow-like.

Joe pushed himself up and stood at attention, saluting. "Paranormal Dimensional Incursion thwarted completely, sir!"

Director Bunsford looked about, nodding. "So I see. And the Dimensional Standard?"

"They never penetrated the final defenses, sir."

"Very good. I shall look forward to your report, but you may take a few hours of rest and get yourself cleaned up. Well, what do you think?" Bunsford gestured at Niels. "Any reservations?"

"Sir, the candidate is a credit to the Bureau of Substandards and exemplifies our finest traditions."

Bunsford blinked, surprised. "I am impressed. Miss Adenaur, do you wish to add anything?"

"He learns and adapts very well, and is extremely quick to pick up on paranormal evidence," Miss Adenaur said primly, refusing to look at Niels.

"Well then, it would appear the matter is settled."

"*What* is settled?" cried Niels, completely confused.

"Why, my boy, we've found a suitable position for you in the Bureau."

Section 4 Recommendations

"...so I did the best I could to warn Joe without revealing anything to Mr. Niels, and once the dimensional portal was triggered I just followed along," said Miss Adenaur. Director Bunsford nodded.

"Yes, it is a pity we have been so short-staffed. Budget cuts, you know," he added to Niels. "We used to be able to train up replacements for upcoming retirements, but these days we have to recruit only when there is an opening. It can be quite nerve-wracking during the changeover. Usually I'm here to pick up the slack, but I had to meet with our alien allies and it always takes hours. Plus their transporter is optimized for their silicon-based life forms and it causes terrible water-retention in humans. But I'm happy to say you did an excellent job and the Dimensional Standard was never in danger."

"Sir, what exactly is a Dimensional Standard? And why did I have to fill out a form to defend it?" asked Niels, the new Sub-director of Dimensionalities.

"Oh, that's our alien allies again. Terribly concerned with respecting tribal traditions of lower cultures, and so on. They first made contact during the Cold War, and they were *quite* impressed with our paperwork system. Don't have anything like it themselves. So, they triggered the Dimensional Defensive System using a complex bio-sensored artificial intelligence in, er, sheet form. If the correct procedure is followed the AI activates the system and immediately destroys all entities not in their home dimensions. The Dimensional Standard is a sort of, well, call it a universal remote for dimensions. Very dangerous to let the wrong people get hold of it, I'm sure you will agree."

"But...why do *we* have it? Why don't these super-powerful aliens guard it or something?"

Director Bunsford sighed. "It is more a matter of *having* to keep it. This is how we earn our allies protection. There are more threats out there than...but that can wait for later. Suffice it to say, by guarding the Dimensional Standard you are in effect protecting the entire planet. Which reminds me, you should sign up for a few of Joe's unarmed combat courses."

Niels digested this in silence for a moment. "You said there were other unusual standards here."

The Director nodded. "Yes, and that will be part of your full briefing. You'll be expected to cover sick days and vacations of the other Sub-directors, after all. Well, let's see, there's the Fermionic sock–if we lose that, you may as well kiss matched pairs of socks goodbye forever. Then there's the One True Fruitcake, and ….

A DARK TRADE IN HEROES

The raid was a wash. Literally. Not only had they failed to catch any of the pirates, something—or someone—had triggered the fire sprinkler system so the entire warehouse was ankle-deep in ice-cold water. Flannery felt his toes go numb and wondered why his right foot felt cold too. It was all metal and plastic now, and he couldn't afford the sensor prosthetic so it must be his imagination.

"Dammit, they got away with the gear again!" Corelli stumbled, cursed, and kicked at something floating in the water.

The warehouse looked bare. A stack of wooden packing crates, some frames made out of old pipe, and a few piles of trash. "You sure we got the right place?"

Corelli picked up a piece of floating paper and handed it to him. "They were printing this somehow. That's what we really need to figure out to shut this operation down. The tech."

The paper looked like an ordinary book page, dense with text. At the top was printed "Priestess of the Space Worm." The title, Flannery guessed. The author's name was missing. "They don't use printers?"

Someone was bringing in evidence bags. Judging from the mess, it was going to be a long night.

"I keep forgetting you're new to the APF. Printers all have anti-piracy capabilities; most people also know that you have to show ID when you buy printer ink. What people don't know is the ink has tracers. These book pirates either don't use printers, or they've hacked them and use illegal ink."

Flannery grabbed a pile of evidence bags and stuck the "Priestess of the Space Worm" page in one of them, bringing out a pen from an inner pocket to write the date, location, and his badge number on the bag label. "Guess I don't read much—never even heard of this book. So why are they pirating it?"

"Who knows?" Corelli hunched his shoulders and looked away. "Come on, or we'll be here all night."

Maybe he'd figure it out if he collected more evidence. The main part of the room had the most people since the light was better. Flannery shook his head and went toward the support pillars with his heavy-duty flashight, the one that made a pretty good truncheon if things got violent. Evidence loved to hide in the dark.

The floor slab was uneven here, and the water barely a thin layer over the concrete. The beam from his flashlight showed several pale blue blocks about a foot long and six inches wide, most of them broken, scattered in the corner. They looked like styrofoam packing forms, only there were markings or a pattern on one side. Flannery bent to pick one up, wincing.

The top of the block was firm and he could grip it, but wherever it had touched the water it crumbled into mush. Even as he watched, the rest of the block began to fall apart. The pattern looked like letters. Carved letters, but somehow wrong. Like a mirror or something. Flannery grimaced at the pale blue goop in his hands and threw it down in disgust. Whatever it had been it wasn't evidence now. He did find more paper pages, enough to fill his hands.

"We out of evidence bags?" He looked around, and stared in shock at the other APF officers simply stuffing bags full of paper without even bothering to write anything. "Hey! You want all that to get thrown out of court? Where did you learn your evidence procedures?"

Corelli scowled at him. "Court? Like we have time for that—none of this is going to court. We're just looking for clues on the print process and the bags are handy. Come on, guys, let's pack it in. They got away with the equipment."

It seemed wrong to just throw the pages away, so Flannery stuffed it in his own gear bag. He still felt he was missing something in this investigation, like he didn't understand the job. And if he screwed this one up, he had no chance of making retirement.

Retirement was the only goal he had left, and now it was just a habit. His patrol partner Buckley had been the one planning it all out. They whiled away long stakeouts and paperwork sessions planning the fishing cabin Buckley was going to live in, and that Flannery would visit. It wasn't that Flannery particularly liked fishing— it would just be a continuation of their usual routine with less shooting and more beer.

Then one dark night Buckley was killed and Flannery's leg shattered, and Flannery had no plans any more except staying alive long enough to retire. And he wasn't going to do that with a cheap reconstructed leg and regular street patrols, so he'd applied for the Arts Protection Force. From what he'd heard, it was mostly desk work and even safer than guarding parking lots. Who ever heard of a book shooting back at someone?

It was early morning by the time they returned to the station and filled out the usual paperwork, and full light when he finally got home, too tired to even drink. He had to go back on duty in a few hours, and he hadn't been sleeping well. To his surprise, he fell asleep almost immediately, and dreamed of a small, imperious little girl with a pet worm wearing a bubble helmet, poling herself to an unknown destination on a pale blue raft.

The dream was vivid enough he pulled out the wad of pages from his bag and read them over his morning coffee. As he had expected, the first two pages had "Priestess of the Space Worm" at the top. Flannery read them with complete puzzlement. Besides a hint of steamy action (all on pages he didn't have) he couldn't make any sense of it. Why was the department wasting time and resources on stopping this glop?

The third page was different. The text at the top read "Lunar Frontier", but still no mention of the author's name.

...if he could reach the reach the rim of the crater, he had a chance. The Selenic mining outfit kept a small supply depot there, and they didn't cut corners like most of the Lunar companies. It would be pressurized and have emergency air canisters. The only problem was it would take Jake three hours on foot to get there, and he had two hours of air remaining—and the bastard that had shot Old Diaz had also nicked his suit.

Devlin clenched his jaw, forcing himself to ignore the stale air and the flickering warning readouts on his helmet display. He was going to get to that depot, and then he was going to hunt the killer down.

Flannery reached blindly for another page from the pile, only to feel the bare surface of the table under his hand. He'd just read ten pages without realizing, caught up in the desperate action. He took a deep breath, savoring the air despite the musty smell of his tiny apartment. He had it good compared to the guy in the suit.

He wondered if the guy survived, if he got to the supply depot in time and found the man who had killed Diaz. The thought returned at odd moments for the rest of the day, and later through the week. While the thought decreased in frequency, it increased in intensity. He *wanted* to know, bad.

If it was a pirated book he ought to be able to find a legal copy, right? Flannery searched for a long time for how to access his local library app. It wasn't like the days when a library was a building and you could go there and ask for help. Now it was some chirpy animated thing that refused to tell him anything about *Lunar Frontier,* or, when he got desperate, *Priestess of the Space Worm.*

Bookstores, maybe. He was pretty sure they still had employees, since that had been part of the legislation that authorized the Arts Protection Force. He had to wait for the end of the workday to do it, and when he got there he glanced over the trendy exterior without enthusiasm. They had the latest, greatest books advertised in the window, all of which had misty covers, foggy cursive titles, and looked about as exciting as cold oatmeal. No spacesuits anywhere.

The only clerk was busy having a voluble chat with a wilting customer. Along one wall was a lookup kiosk. Maybe he could use that instead of waiting. Flannery studied the screen for a moment to figure it out and then typed in the title.

No records found.

Shrugging, he tried "Priestess of the Space Worm". That didn't come up with anything either. He had no choice but to wait for the clerk. He turned around, noticing quick movement out of the corner of his eye. Somebody in a faded purple jacket, but he couldn't see them now.

The clerk, however, had seen him. She was bright and bubbly and didn't so much listen to his question as stop talking to catch her breath. "First, let's look at your authorization status." She held out her hand expectantly for his data card.

"I'm just looking for a book," Flannery protested. "Lunar Frontier." Maybe he should have left his uniform on for this.

"Oh no, I can't do that," she said with what was probably intended to be a roguish wink. "Are you trying to get me in trouble?"

"Trouble? All those reader guideline regulations are voluntary." He *had* read the legislation, not that his department did much with the legal book trade.

It didn't stop her, but her smile got a trifle sharp. "Yes sir, totally voluntary but all Reader Guardian bookstores comply fully with the guidelines and we are RG certified." She pointed to the orange and blue symbol prominently displayed on the counter. "I think we are up to 98% store compliance now, so all readers can have a truly *enriching* literary experience."

Flannery handed his card with a sigh and she went behind the counter to use the secure reader. He looked around while waiting, wondering if the store was always this empty. A glimpse of color caught his attention— someone in a faded purple jacket was standing in front of the community bulletin board pinning up a small white card.

"Sir?" Flannery spun back to face the counter. "It's great that you are starting an interest in reading," chirped the clerk, with a forceful smile. "We have all the recommended introductory books, and a discount program for new customers. Once you have the fundamental understanding of literary analysis you can begin personal guided exploration. However, you have to complete the required reading before we can sell you anything not on the approved list."

"Wait, can't I just pick the book I want?"

Her smile became more rigid. "We want you to have the best literary experience possible. How could you possibly know what books are good when you are just starting out? What if you picked the wrong book?

We spend a great deal of time carefully curating our selection to expand the reader's understanding of the important topics of the day. Based on your profile, I would recommend starting with "Standard Useful Lives", a collection of short stories about ordinary people doing ordinary things and reflecting on them."

"Do any of these people go to the moon?"

The clerk blinked at him. "Well, that's hardly an ordinary life, wouldn't you agree? According to the latest industry studies, reading about people with abilities and experiences different from your own will only cause stress and self-esteem issues. Now would you like a copy? Or would you prefer..." her voice lost its forced cheerfulness, "the electronic version?"

"I'll have to come back later," Flannery mumbled and made his escape. It was clear nothing interesting had ever been in that store. But what had the clerk said about required reading? Who the hell cared about that?

He started to walk home, feeling depressed. It was like a promised treat that vanished just before he got it, or a piece of cake that looked great but tasted like sawdust. *I wonder what the spacesuit guy would do*, he found himself wondering. Not getting bent out of shape about a stupid story, that's for sure.

Something was bothering him. The street, the people...oh yeah. He was being followed. Not very well, but someone was definitely following him. He even switched streets to make sure. Maybe his beat cop skills were still useful after all.

He pulled a fast corner fade and saw a familiar purple jacket go by, and his eyebrows went up. Not one of his criminal acquaintances, then. Time to find out some things.

"Looking for me?"

Purple jacket jumped and spun around. It was a woman with wispy, straw-blonde hair and a thin face. She recovered quick from her surprise, he had to give her that.

"I heard you at the bookstore." Her pale blue eyes were cold and hard. "I also saw the ID you flashed when you took out your data card. Why is a book cop looking for unlicensed books at a *bookstore*, of all places?"

Unlicensed? "Why wouldn't I look for books in a bookstore?" And why was she mad about it? Maybe she was off her nut—but his instincts said not. He'd seen enough crazy to know. "And it's not for work. Well, I came across a book on the job, on a raid. The pirates were printing it. I read a bit and thought I'd get a legal copy."

The woman gaped, then burst out laughing. "*Legal?* Are you sure you're a book cop? Asking for unlicensed books at a bookstore is almost as dumb as searching for them at the library." She paused, looking at him narrowly. "You did, didn't you? How dumb are you? You'll be lucky if you don't get arrested—although it would be funny for them to grab one of their own people. Seriously, how can you not know about this? How long have you been a book cop, anyway?"

"I've been with the Arts Protection Force for three months," Flannery said, speaking the name of the department slow and clear. He was pissed at her for figuring out he was a new guy so fast, and pissed at himself for being obvious. "Before that I was a beat cop for twenty-eight years."

"Oh." She frowned. "OK, so that's why...hang on. If it isn't for work, why are you doing this? I head that twit in the bookstore trying to get you in the indoctrination program, but that's for people who haven't bought books before."

"I'm not a reader. Last book I read that wasn't for my job was in high school." So why was he so interested? "This *Lunar Frontier* thing was...different. I kinda forgot I was reading, you know? Like it was real. I guess I just want to know how it ended. If the guy survived and all."

He looked up. Her expression had changed from anger to shock. "You...you liked *Lunar Frontier?*"

"Yeah. It was interesting. Made me wonder about what it would be like living on the moon. Wonder why we never went back."

She sighed. "Look. It's pretty clear you don't know what's really happening. *Lunar Frontier* wasn't pirated, because it was never officially published."

But I read it... How could it not be published? It certainly seemed real enough. Then what she had said hit him. "So I'm never gonna know how it ends." Flannery sighed. It was a grey day and his whole life now felt drained of color too. Except for the woman in the faded purple jacket.

"Depends on how far you are willing to go." Her voice had gone soft and quiet, and she took a step closer, staring at him. "You said you found some pages—it was being printed by somebody, right? You just have to find out who. Oh, and convince them that a book cop should be trusted not to rat them out for making unlicensed books. That's the hard part." She gave him a tight smile.

"You'll have to prove yourself. What they are doing is dangerous if they get caught, so you'll have to offer something they really want to even talk to them."

"Yeah? Like what? Money? I'm so poor even the roaches left for somewhere they could eat regular."

She shook her head. "I'm thinking something only you can get. Supposedly you APF guys store a lot of the stuff you confiscate. You find a copy of *Tales of Valent,* you can trade that for anything you want. Nobody has a copy of that. I hear," she added hastily.

Flannery stifled a chuckle. It was pretty clear to him she was part of whatever this was, and she was just as bad at hiding this as she was at tailing someone. But he knew the rules, and one was to play along with the spin the informant handed you no matter how ridiculous it was.

"Say I find it. Then what?"

"Go to the flea market by the river. Ask around for Skaith Vintage Artifacts, and when you find it tell whoever's in charge you've got an exchange for Rita. My name's not Rita, so don't bother checking up on me, OK?"

"Got it." Flannery turned to leave, wondering what he'd gotten involved in and whether he should just pretend it never happened.

"Hey, book cop." The woman not named Rita was behind him now, but he didn't turn around. "Try not to be such an idiot, OK? Asking questions like you did can get people killed. People like the person who wrote *Lunar Frontier*." That made him stop. He hadn't even thought of that, that a real human being had written the words he'd read. "Just...don't cause trouble."

"Got it." He walked away.

Flannery agonized over what to do during a long sleepless night, until he realized there was a chance he could get what he wanted without Rita. Assuming this evidence storeroom existed, he might be able to find *Lunar Frontier* there. When he asked it turned out the APF did have an evidence room for bulk items. They were in large boxes labeled with the date and crime scene ID, but no other itemization beyond that. It was sloppy police work. He got in the first time claiming he wanted to add the papers he'd taken home "by mistake," and once he saw how the process worked he went back more often, waiting until shift change so no one else would be present. Quickly lifting the lid, he'd riffle through the papers.

Some of the contents were loose sheets, like he'd

found in the raid. Other times they were crudely bound into actual books, some even with fake covers that seemed to be from "approved" books. But as the weeks went by and he methodically went through the boxes, he saw no sign of *Lunar Frontier*.

Finally he reached the last set of boxes in a far corner. They were dusty and the date on the boxes was years prior. The first one had loose pages of several oddly titled books and, for the first time, the author name. Goya Andare. Flannery wondered why the rest he'd seen never mentioned the author.

The second box had a tattered, but complete, bound copy of *Tales of Valent*. He took a deep breath, hoping his stomach would settle and opened the last box. More Goya Andare, but no *Lunar Frontier*. If he wanted it, he would have to deal with Rita. And he wanted it, bad.

Hands shaking, Flannery tucked the volume in the small of his back, held in place by his belt and covered by his jacket. It wouldn't be noticeable with all the gear he carried. He quickly stepped out of the evidence room and shut the door.

He'd never been a shady cop; never taken a bribe or a favor or broken the rules. Now here he was, stealing evidence and he was only worried about being caught.

What had happened to him? In his heart, he guessed, he really didn't think unauthorized books were a crime. Who did it hurt? Where was the loss caused by *Priestess of the Space Worm?* Well, besides minor brain damage.

"Hey, Flannery!"

He hadn't checked the hallway. He always checked the hallway. Heart pounding, Flannery turned. Corelli was looking at him, expressionless. "I wondered why you were never around your desk much lately. What's going on?"

He could feel his face heat. What possible explanation could he give, except for the true one? The stories. Somebody had to make that stuff up, make it believable. He needed to do the same thing. He could hear her voice now...*don't cause trouble.*

"It's just...you guys know so much about this and I'm new to all of it. I'm not pulling my weight. I want to be useful, see...and I thought if I look at the evidence, get to know it, right? Maybe I might see something helpful. At least learn the basics. What kind of a cop am I if I can't even help my team?" Flannery hung his head, warming to his role.

His partner ate it up. "Hey, don't feel bad. You're not going to pick up my years of experience in a month, after all. Don't worry, Flannery. You'll get used to it." Corelli slapped him on the back, narrowly missing the stolen book. "Find anything useful in there? Come on, the rest of us are going out for a beer. You'll learn more from them than from that pile of crap."

Flannery somehow managed to keep up the humble new guy act all through the beer-drinking session. The book cops all had a veneer of arrogance, especially noticeable in their bragging tales of the early days of the Act when they arrested pirates and shut down printing operations, traced file-sharing sites and set up sting operations. Flannery was beginning to understand why Rita had been so wary and suspicious of him. He hadn't known they arrested people for "material assistance to piracy", which seemed to include being in possession of illegal printing supplies or pirated books with intent to sell.

None of the book cops seemed to care about books or reading.

That didn't mean Flannery wanted to keep the incriminating evidence any longer than he had to. The riverside flea market ran Thursday through Saturday, with an eclectic mix of hawkers and pushcart vendors. Asking for Skaith Vintage Artifacts got him sent along the length of the riverfront, until he finally reached a grimy alley with a peeling roll-up door on one side.

A slouching, scowling young man in a hoodie watched him go in, then closed the roll-up door from the outside. Flannery peered through the gloom, trying to slow his hammering pulse. What the hell had he gotten into? Two big men walked up silently. One frisked him professionally while the other stood just outside of reach with a baseball bat. Flannery could make out a faded tattoo on one arm that read "Tolle Lege" in gothic script.

They found the book, of course. The frisker opened the cover, stone-faced, then whistled. "Damn. We finally got it."

"It's an exchange. For Rita." Flannery was sweating and hoping it wasn't visible. She'd said the book was valuable, but were they just going to take it?

"Yeah. She told us you might show." The tattooed man smiled. "Didn't think you would. Glad I was wrong. Hope you don't have plans for the evening."

"I just want *Lunar Frontier...*"

Tattoo guy was suddenly in front of him, one hand grabbing the front of Flannery's shirt and the other raising the baseball bat. "She also told us who you work for. So you are gonna sit tight until we get this done, just in case. Don't worry, you'll get your book—as long as we don't get raided before we finish."

Flannery was escorted to a small room in the back and the door locked. There was a ratty sofa, a bent metal folding chair, a stepstool, and a pile of old carpet remnants. On one wall was a faded travel poster and a cracked mirror. The only light came from the frosted glass panel in the door, although Flannery could see a faint gleam where the wall met the drop ceiling. It looked like one of the ceiling panels was broken, which gave him an idea. He didn't want to get caught unawares by anybody, not the pirates or the APF. Not until he got his book.

He wrapped some of the carpet around the metal folding chair and swung it against the mirror until it broke. He waited to see if the sound had attracted attention, then picked up one of the larger fragments. Using the stepstool, Flannery wedged the mirror fragment in the ceiling gap to get a view of the outside.

The previously empty room looked like a kicked-over ant hill. In the middle the surly hoodie kid was feeding a sheet of paper into a slim rectangular device connected to a laptop. He'd grab the sheet on the other side and flip it over to feed it in again. Then he took another sheet from a pile, a pile that looked pretty much the same thickness and size as the book Flannery brought. Every few minutes the kid would take out and hand off a small chipdrive to someone who then ran out of the building at full speed. The atmosphere was excited yet tense. He wished he could hear what people were saying, but they were being careful to lower their voices.

New activity at the door that got everyone's attention suddenly. A raid? No, they seemed to be expecting the new arrivals, who were carrying a series of what looked like fast food delivery boxes. They stacked them near another strange device an older man had been cobbling together. It looked like junk to Flannery, but it also had a laptop connected to it.

Then someone opened one of the fast food boxes, and Flannery felt the dots starting to connect. The boxes didn't have food. They were completely packed with blue blocks that looked real familiar, except these didn't have any patterns on the surface.

After the old guy and his junk device were through with them, they did. Flannery frowned, trying to remember. At the raid, the blocks looked like they'd been engraved with letters that weren't letters. What the hell were these people doing?

The engraved blocks were handed off to another setup, about ten frames that also looked like they were constructed of scrap pipe and just big enough to fit one of the blue blocks in the base. Each had a handle, and a wire mesh basket with blank paper stacked in a pile. Flannery blinked. He'd seen those frames before somewhere.

As soon as a frame had its blue block, somebody in the crowd grabbed the handle and another showed up with a roller and a spray bottle with something black inside. They sprayed the gunk on the roller and wiped it on the block. Turning the crank dropped a sheet of paper and then a plate that sandwiched the paper between it and the blue block smeared with black goop.

We need the tech, Corelli had said. Printing tech that didn't use electronic printers. No wonder the APF had never found anything. Even if they did, it would look like junk to them. And then he remembered the raid where he'd found the pages of *Lunar Frontier.* The frames made of pipe—they *had* seen some of the tech, they just hadn't realized it.

The tables now had piles of papers with text on them. Another assembly line was putting the actual books together and stacking them back in the fast food boxes. As soon as one was full a runner grabbed it and headed out the door. It hadn't even been an hour since Flannery was locked in the office. These guys knew what they were doing—it was a pro operation. So how many other books were they making, in secret? It wasn't just *Tales of Valent*. Clearly there was demand for these stories. Enough to risk getting arrested for it.

At some point the kid in the hoodie had vanished, along with the laptop and the device. All that was left was the original copy of *Tales of Valent* on the table. The old guy carving the page blocks had disassembled his gear and was stowing it in various worn duffle bags, which also got the multiple-runner treatment. If any of them got caught, it wouldn't look like much. Certainly not a pirate printing device.

Flannery caught a glimpse of purple near the entrance. People were crowding around so he couldn't see much until they shifted a bit. Rita. She had a big grin on her face and people were slapping her on the back and hugging her. It looked like a low-rent celebrity meeting. The big tattoo guy came up and handed her a book from his back pocket but it looked different than the ones they'd been making. Rita opened it, took out a pen, and scribbled something before handing it back.

She said something and the guy pointed back to the office with Flannery.

Oops. Time for me to look bored and ignorant.

He dropped down and hid the fragment of mirror before taking a seat and slouching like he was dozing off. The door creaked open.

"You guys gonna give me my book now?" Flannery glared, then put on his best impression of complete surprise. "Rita?"

She shoved the original Valent volume at him. "Here. Good as new, or good as when it showed up. Thanks," she mumbled, her face going red. "We'd...we were afraid it was lost forever."

Flannery took the book, realizing he could put it back in the evidence room and nobody would ever know. "That's great, but this isn't the book I want."

Tattoo guy made a choking noise and Rita smacked him on the shoulder. "Yeah, yeah I got your payment. One copy of *Lunar Frontier*. Please don't read it at work, OK? Or leave it out where your book cop buddies can see. The author doesn't want to go to prison." She took out another book from an inside pocket of her purple jacket. The cover was plain but it looked brand new. Flannery grabbed it and took a look, heart pounding. He'd finally got it, the whole thing. He'd find out the ending.

"It's even got the author's glyph," Tattoo guy said, proud like it was a car with leather seats or an overclocked engine. "You got your promised payout and more."

"What's a glyph?" Flannery followed them out of the office. Nobody else was there. The open space was completely empty now, without even a scrap of paper left from the busy book fabrication.

Tattoo guy took out the book from his pocket and opened the cover. A scrawled symbol took up most of the blank page at the front. "Used to be signatures, but the book cops used that to identify writers."

"Is that why they don't even put their names on the books? That Andare guy did, though."

The tattoo guy snarled and Rita's face hardened. "Yeah, exactly. You know what happened to Andare? He didn't even last a month after getting arrested. They were careful, no bruises or broken bones. But we...the fans, we knew he needed meds for his heart. We also know he never got them in jail. They really wanted Andare gone, see. His books were exactly what the law was trying to stop. They made you think, and dream.

They were *adventure*."

It had never occurred to Flannery that there might be other books like *Lunar Frontier*. Maybe he should try this *Tales of Valent* thing before putting it back.

All three of them carefully checked the street outside before leaving. It was dark and a bit chilly now, and nobody was in sight. Tattoo guy nodded and silently slipped into the shadows. Flannery headed back the way he had come and made no attempt to hide. For one thing, he knew someone, probably Tattoo guy, would be following him to make sure he didn't have an APF tail. So he was a little surprised to see Rita walking beside him, all nonchalant like she'd decided to go for a stroll at midnight for no reason.

"There's other books by the person who wrote *Lunar Frontier*," she said, looking straight ahead.

Flannery kept a poker face. "Since nobody uses a name and they aren't approved, how would I know?"

"Maybe I'd tell you."

"Why?"

"Keep you quiet." Rita turned her head and gave him a look out of narrowed eyes. "I don't know how much you saw back there but you were breathing pretty deep for a guy just waking up from a nap."

Well, shit. Flannery kept his face blank. "So why didn't you tell the muscle to take care of me before he left?"

"I keep asking myself that." She was silent for a moment. "Maybe because of why you got into this. Because you wanted to read that book so bad. You gonna tell the book cops anything?"

"No way I can tell them without getting myself in trouble, and you know it. Besides...I don't see why this is wrong. Nobody's bleeding. Nothing got stolen, really. Guess that makes me a lousy book cop, huh."

She grinned. "World needs more lousy book cops in my opinion. Say. You see any other books when you were looking for *Valent*?"

"Sure. There were a bunch by that Andare guy. And some handwritten stuff, but I don't know if it was a full book or not—"

"*Notes?* He left notes?" Rita had stopped and was staring at him.

He stared back. "Same deal as before?"

"Same deal."

They started again walking in the gloom.

"How many other books from the *Lunar Frontier* guy?"

Rita chuckled. "Five. Oh, and a sequel is in the works. According to the author."

"Really. You know him?" Flannery winced. "Sorry. Forget I asked."

"How do you think I got your copy with the glyph?"

"Thanks. Tell him he writes good stuff."

"I'll pass it along." Rita didn't seem mad. Instead, she had a small smile curling the corners of her mouth. "He'll be happy to hear it. Really happy," she said softly. "He loved Andare's writing a lot. He owes you a big favor for saving *Tales of Valent*."

Huh. He saved a book. Maybe he was a good book cop after all. Not the one the APF wanted, but the one the books needed. To protect, and serve.

Flannery smiled. When he retired he'd have more time to read. Finally, something to look forward to.

****

"Space opera, as every reader doubtless knows, is a pejorative term often applied to a story that has an element of adventure. Over the decades, brilliant and

talented new writers appear, receiving great acclaim, and each and every one of them can be expected to write at least one article stating flatly that the day of space opera is over and done, thank goodness, and that henceforth these crude tales of interplanetary nonsense will be replaced by whatever type of story that writer happens to favor — closet dramas, psychological dramas, sex dramas, etc., but by God important dramas, containing nothing but Big Thinks. Ten years late, the writer in question may or may not still be around, but the space opera can be found right where it always was, sturdily driving its dark trade in heroes."

— Leigh Brackett, The Best of Planet Stories 1

WOLF OF SHADOWS

The cold, red silk fell like water over Donn's hand as he moved the drapery aside from the tower window. It was a prison with no iron bars—magic warded the windows and the only door; the walls were of stone. Knowing the fate planned for him, he would have preferred to stay in the dungeons. Could she even find him here? That was his only hope of survival. A slender hope at best, but his life had been in danger since the day he was born. If his half-brother Tormod had not found a use for him, he would be dead now.

Donn was not his real name. Royal bastards were never given true names. Donn meant "the dark one," a reference to his unusual dark hair. His reflection in the diamond panes of the window was just a pale face, surrounded by shadow, as he gazed out from the tower to the forest and mountains beyond. Waiting, and despairing. *She promised she would return ...*

He shivered, his breath visible in the cold. The clothes he wore were much too thin for the chilly room—cast-off formal attire, long out of fashion but still smelling faintly of the musky perfume used by the former owner. Tormod had ordered Donn be dressed well to impress the envoy of the desert people, and reassure them of his royal blood. If he were seen in his usual rags, it might provoke awkward questions—and more importantly, the loss of the horses the desert people had brought in trade.

A glimpse of motion outside made him stiffen, and Donn leaned closer, staring intently through the icy window panes. A grey wolf stood at the edge of the dark forest, barely visible in the shadows next to the moonlit snow. Its jaws was open, as if it laughed. Donn's breath frosted the window, obscuring his view. Impatiently he scrubbed the frost away, ignoring the warning twinges from the wards, but when he looked again the wolf had gone. He grabbed the window latch in desperation, but agonizing pain from the fully active wards soon made him release it.

She could open the wards. He'd helped her do it, and she had promised. And he had believed her.

Closing his eyes, he drew his knees up and rested his face against them. He should never have believed he could escape the castle. If she had not come, he would not have been caught so soon. If she had not come, he would not have hoped.

The sound of approaching footsteps alerted him that he was no longer alone, and he stared stonily out the window. The glass reflected the approaching figure of a minor courtier famous for gossip. The cruelty of Tormod meant the wards of Donn's prison were only for him. Everyone else could come and go as they pleased.

"But a short time until you wed the desert leader! At least you will be well away from all the snow and cold,. You must be impatient to go."

Donn said nothing, hoping the man would take offense and leave.

"And of course, as befits your...connection to the royal house, you will be her principal husband. I can't imagine the others, barbarians as they are, will be serious competition even for you."

This promising lead, and several others, were equally ignored. Unable to pry the smallest tidbit of information from him, the courtier's spite flared.

"They are ignorant, the desert people. What will you do when she learns you have no name?"

This bitter parting cut won only a listless glance, and the courtier left in great annoyance.

Donn sighed. The courtier was correct; the desert people knew little of the customs here. The courtier was equally ignorant of theirs—unlike Donn. He had taken refuge many times in the dusty rooms of the archives, where the members of the court never went. He devoured any account of life outside the castle walls, desperate for escape if only in his mind. One such account was of the customs of the desert people.

He would be treated kindly, lack no luxury—once they had blinded him to prevent his escape. And after two years the desert leader would require a new principal husband. Or, more correctly translated, "blood sacrifice."

#

The hunter had come in the season of Redleaf, guiding a storyteller who had lost his way in Longwall Forest. Her profession was clear from the longbow and shaggy grey pelt she wore over her shoulders.

It was the fourth year of the king's madness, and

only tales, new tales, could calm his rages. All the corners of the kingdom sent their best tellers of tales, but fewer and fewer came each year. This storyteller came from a village of the fisher people, on a bare stony island. An old, twisted man, he seemed lost so far from the sound of the sea.

Donn had felt restless that day, sensing an unsettling disturbance in the atmosphere of the castle. He traced that disturbance to the Audience chamber, where the king gibbered and thrashed on the throne, tied down with heavy silken cords. Tormod, the unofficial regent, stood below the dais as the travelers were brought in, the old man leaning on the hunter woman. Donn watched them from the concealing shadows of the gallery pillars even though it was dangerous for him to go so close. In his sixteen years he had learned that it was always safer to stay out of sight, to steal his food from the kitchen instead of taking his place at meals, to sleep anywhere but his bed.

The Audience was not so much a room as a clearing in the thicket of columns that supported the dome. Clusters of slender pillars stood about in such a way that there was no straight path to any doorway, nor was any path indicated as more important than another. As the hunter went by his hiding place, a small breeze, carrying the faint scent of pine and woodsmoke, cut through the must and florid perfume of the court. *That must be what Outside smells like.* Donn shifted to see her more clearly. Her rough, ash-white hair had bone beads woven in it. He could almost see the invisible lines of power bend around her disturbing presence.

There were others with business before the storyteller and his hunter escort, so Donn had time to watch them both. The hunter stood out from the gaudy court brocades and silks like a barbaric ghost, all in shades of grey and white. A black bow was slung across her back, a belt quiver held black-fletched arrows. He tried to imagine what it would be like Outside, never being surrounded by walls, but his imagination failed him. He was certain, however, that he would prefer it.

He had stared some time when she suddenly turned her head and looked in his direction, the only motion during her long wait. He froze, his heart hammering. It was impossible she had seen him, the shadows were too thick, but still he found himself moving cautiously to another group of pillars further back.

When at last their turn came, the hunter remained silent as the old man quavered his name and business.

Tormod thanked him urbanely, asked him to begin that very day, commanded him to ask for anything he required—while his gaze never left the hunter. Donn inhaled sharply. The dark aura that he always saw about Tormod had increased, and seemed to roil around him.

Tormod asked the hunter to name a payment, but she shook her head. He looked at her with narrowed eyes. "Then you must enjoy the hospitality my father offers, as befits your service to him." He gestured his dismissal. As she walked away the storyteller turned his dismayed glance from the crazed king to her, despairing, as if he finally comprehended the nature of his task.

As the hunter left the Audience Tormod gestured to a guard, and Donn saw his lips form the word "gate." His heart hammering, Donn darted away from the central court through the maze of columns, slowing his pace when he found her. Like all newcomers to the castle, she had been caught by the deliberate confusion of the columned halls and deceptive corridors, and she stood at the crossroads of several passageways which had nothing to distinguish them. Once again she seemed to sense his presence, and turned to face him.

Her eyes were forest green, like jade, set under winging back brows. Around her neck a bone gorget, inscribed with runes, hung from a leather thong. Looking at them, he felt the hairs on his neck rise and a chill run over him. As he stared, wordless, a flicker of amusement passed over her face.

"You must run, hide," he gasped finally. "Tormod will be creating a sending soon to hold you."

"Why would he do this? I did nought but bring the old man." Her voice had an odd, burring lilt to it.

Donn gestured wildly. "I don't know what he wants; does it matter? I could see it building around him, and he has sent a guard to find you as well. You have to get away from the Audience."

"Show me to the gate." All amusement had left her face.

"He's ordered the gate closed by now. You can't get out." Suddenly he felt the itching, crawling sensation that preceded a sending. He whirled, and saw the almost-specks from the edge of his vision. "Run!" He darted for one of the passages that led away from the spell, grabbing her arm as he went. She pulled free, but followed close behind.

The passage he had chosen was not the best for avoiding a quick sending. We have to get up, out of its path. Down this corridor, the second door...there!

An addition to the castle, centuries ago, had met the older section where the floors were at different levels. An old doorway, leading to a small room piled with rubble and unused for centuries, now stood more than halfway up the wall. Enough of the room remained to be useful, though, especially after Djeragh had.... He pulled his mind angrily away from the memory.

"In there!" he gasped, indicating the hole near the ceiling as they dashed into the room. He leaped, grabbed, and pulled himself in the hiding place and out of the way. The hunter followed, negotiating the entrance with fluid grace.

Donn wiggled back to the mouth of the hole and looked out cautiously. In no time at all, he sensed the not-quite-seen speckles of the sending floating down the corridor. They had been lucky—a few seconds more and it would have found them. The sending floated lazily, washing nearly halfway up the wall. Tormod was using a considerable amount of power, then. Donn put his head on his arms and tried to recover his breath.

"What is it, the thing you run from?" He thought he saw a flash of green light from the darkness where she was.

"A spell. To find and hold people."

"I saw nothing."

He sighed. "Most can't. The only reason I've stayed alive so long is that I can." He peered out again. "I see the power, I think. Tormod's got a lot around him, always. There's power in the charm you wear. I just see it, and know it's different."

When the sending dissipated, they moved cautiously out into the corridor. At the hunter's insistence, Donn led her through the mazelike passageways, down stairs concealed in corners, through narrow, unimportant looking doors, to the courtyard of the outer bailey. The door that led to the courtyard was so small they had to bend double to go through, and they emerged behind a wall that hid a malodorous pile of garbage.

The hunter stood, blinking in the light, and looked about. The gates were indeed closed, and soldiers manned the postern towers and stood before the gates themselves. Other travelers, caught unawares, protested fruitlessly.

"A strange hospitality, that keeps a guest regardless," she commented.

"Tormod loves to wield the power he holds," Donn said quietly. "He wants to keep you here."

"I would be in the trees again."

"There are some trees within the walls. Not many, but...I'll show you."

Always watchful, he led her past the old, crumbling stables and around the oldest castle tower to what had once been a pleasure garden. When the outer wall had been built, centuries ago, it encircled the craggy top of the hill the castle rested on, enclosing also a spring and a small grove of trees. The grove had diminished over time but the spring remained, with clear, icy water welling up from deep within the earth. It was rarely visited, Donn knew, but still they waited in the shadows as the twilight deepened until it was clear the grove was abandoned.

The hunter dipped her cupped hands in the water and drank. Wiping her mouth on her sleeve, she gazed about the tiny grove. "The trees have scarce power to live, here. It is no good place to bide."

"There aren't many here who choose to stay. Those with power to leave, do so. I would," he added bitterly. She turned her gaze to him.

"You have power," she said, her voice matter-of-fact. "Else your mind would have been broken as the Seated Chieftain's was. The darkness in this place can be felt."

Donn did not know how to respond to this. *She means the King,* he realized, astonished. *This place drove him mad?* Yet another reason to get Outside.

"Where do you live, then?"

"No one place. Wherever the forest runs."

"Because you hunt....what?"

She smiled, showing strong white teeth. "Many things." He swallowed, his throat gone dry. "I thank you for your aid," she said. "Tell me what you fear in this place, and I will do what I can to aid you in turn. Why does this Tormod wish you ill?"

Donn gave a humorless laugh, and collapsed by the well. The hunter sat more gracefully in the shadow of the trees, seeming relaxed, but he sensed her alertness.

"Do you know how the new king is chosen? Tormod has several brothers, each as dangerous as he is. After the death of the king there are sudden illnesses, accidents—and only one heir survives. But before the old king dies, the heirs practice on the bastards. They must be discreet...we are supposed to be half-royal, after all, and one heir would use such a mistake to banish another. And sometimes we fight back. My sister Djeragh took Tormod's best assassin with her when he pushed her from the walls..." He stopped, unable to continue. A distant part of him marveled at how sharp the pain was still, how his heart still wailed her name.

"I am sorry for your sister's death. May her spirit be free," the hunter said, gently. The light had vanished from the sky, and he could no longer see her face in the shadows. "Are there other killers, then, that you fear?"

"Tormod believes the king will die soon. He keeps his men close by him now, and so do the others. His magic is the strongest, but even he cannot afford to create sendings at whim. They will not seek me out, I think, until the king dies."

"And then?"

"And then I die too."

The next morning the hunter was nowhere to be found. The gates had not been opened, and troops of guards searched throughout the castle. Donn watched the unusual activity fearfully, afraid someone might have seen them together and blame him for her escape. He took great care to stay out of view, even going to a high nook in a ruined tower to avoid a possible sending. He wondered if the hunter had achieved the impossible and successfully escaped the castle.

That evening Donn found himself by the well again.

He stared blindly at the gently rippling water, wondering where the hunter had gone, what it would be like to be free to travel the forest.

A faint sound of stealthy movement roused him from his musing, and he looked up to see a moving shadow in the shade of the grove. A shadow that fit the shape of a wolf, and in a blaze of fear he scrambled to his feet and ran. He lost his footing on the slippery rock by the well and fell hard. He rolled to face his attacker...but the wolf was gone. The hunter was leaning against the oldest oak, looking at him in mild puzzlement.

"The wolf! Where is it?"

Her mouth twitched. "I have seen no wolf. Are you hurt?"

He got up slowly. His side was sore where he had fallen on the rock, but he was otherwise unharmed. Embarrassment replaced his earlier fear. Why had he been so sure there was a wolf? A wolf could never scale the massive walls, or enter by the only gate. He hadn't actually *seen* it, only a shadow...which must have been the hunter herself.

"The castle guard are looking for you. How did you avoid them?"

She shrugged, reaching down to pick up something ragged-looking from the ground. "I did not choose they should find me."

His further questions were simply ignored. Moving further into the shadow of the grove, she prepared a fire. It was tiny, and gave no smoke, but it was enough to cook the birds she had brought. Donn's fingers were greasy when they were done, and he was sure he had swallowed several small feathers, but it was the best food he had ever eaten.

"Have you tried to leave?" the hunter said suddenly, into the silence.

Donn stared at her, scornful. "How? There is only one gate to the outer bailey and curtain wall, and it is always guarded. There is a spell there, too; I've seen it. The walls are said to be bespelled as well."

"Yet birds fly in at will," she noted, twirling a feather between her fingers.

He shrugged, irritated. "Maybe the spell is for humans. Anyway, I can't climb it to find out, it's too high and smooth." Then, suspicion slowly dawning, "You can get out, can't you. That's why they didn't find you today. How did you do it?"

"I could not get out." Her voice was sharp. "I have

ways of concealment, but they are not ways I can teach you." She turned away, pulling the wolf pelt around her shoulders more tightly. Concealing the gorget around her neck.

"Is it a charm that you wear? Is that how you remain hidden?" Her green eyes narrowed at him. "I'm not trying to pry at your secrets. I just...even if I can't escape, I want to stay alive."

The hunter's posture relaxed. "It was made for me alone, bound to my name," she said, her fingers touching the bone gorget. "If you wore it, it would do nothing for you."

They were silent for a while, then Donn asked hesitantly, "What is it like, Outside?"

He managed to find out more about her, despite her laconic replies. Her people did not give out their true names to outsiders; she did not seem to think his lack of name worthy of comment. The name she used was Bayn. Her knife was some lustrous black stone that had been chipped to form an edge, and the points of her arrows were made of the same material. Sometimes the firelight would reflect in her eyes as a green flame, like a night-beast's would. He fell asleep wondering why.

He woke by the well next morning, stiff and chilled.

There was no sign of Bayn, the fire, or the birds they had eaten. He drifted about the hidden ways of the castle once more, feeling confused and edgy, as if something important were about to happen. When night fell he went to the well, carefully seating himself to face away from the grove, looking only at the water.

Not much longer after that he found Bayn had appeared beside him. She was even more taciturn than before, and restless.

"Why is it that the storytellers are brought here? Why does this Tormod care if the Seated Chieftain raves or not?" she asked finally.

Donn raised his eyes from the rippled surface of the water. "Because of the wards. They are bound to the king, linked to him. When he raves, they become dangerous and unpredictable. They can overpower the castle wards and then no one can leave, not even Tormod."

Bayn stared at him. "What wards are these, that the king has?"

"Wards of personal protection. He cannot be killed by steel or magic, and the wards can also join with other magics to further shield him."

"Other magics—this could include the castle

wards? Like the shield above?"

Donn shrugged. "Of course. That is what has happened, at least at the gate. I'm not sure about anything above the castle."

Her fist struck her palm, and her eyes gleamed with green fire. "I am sure. It would not respond to Tormod's name. Quickly, what is the name of the king?"

He stared, not understanding. "His regnal name is Koron..."

She mouthed the word, then shook her head. "No, the name he was given at birth. His true name."

Donn wrinkled his forehead. "I have never heard it. He was king well before I was...wait." Memories were coming to him, of names, a scroll. Now he remembered. He had seen an old genealogy in the archives, from the time of the king before. "It may be written down."

In a sudden movement she was on one knee before him, her face grim. "I must know this name. True names have power, did you know this? With his true name, I can open the shield."

"But...but the gate will still be guarded, and there is no other way through the walls."

The corners of Bayn's mouth turned up. "May they continue to think so. *Where can I find the name?*"

The archive was near the central keep. If a sending was invoked, even he would not be able to escape it. If she entered the castle again, Tormod's sendings would find her. If he went instead, he risked being found by the searching guards.

I must go. Even if I cannot escape, she will be free.

Donn stood, feeling cold. "I will find it for you."

Soldiers were everywhere inside the castle. Donn nearly abandoned the attempt several times, crouched in the shadows and holding his breath. There was nowhere to hide near the archives, unfortunately, and a soldier was patrolling the corridor. Donn waited until the man was at the far end, back turned, and then ran with all the speed he could muster.

Inside the archive, he leaned against the closed door and tried to stifle his gasping breath. If the soldier had seen the door closing or had heard anything, he was done for. But as time passed and no shouts were heard, Donn shuddered with relief and forced himself to move.

It was dangerous for him to stay too long. A sending for Bayn would not hold him, but Tormod would still know he was there. Donn rummaged through the scrolls, not caring if they were disordered. With the dust so thick, it was clear no one had been here in a long time and no change would be noticed.

Finally he found it, just as he remembered. An old scroll, with the red caps indicating a royal record, the leather ties ragged with age. He opened it up with haste, running his finger down the branches of the genealogy, remembering this king had been the oldest of his brothers. And there it was. *Rieghe*.

Donn opened the door of the archive a crack, listening for the sound of footsteps. The corridor was silent, and after a moment he dared to look out. The soldier was gone.

Hardly daring to believe his luck, he ran. It was only when he had nearly reached the crowded bustle of the courtyard that he realized he had not seen *any* soldiers—and then it was too late. They were behind him, and coming through the courtyard gate, and there was nowhere to hide or run.

They dragged him out to the courtyard, yelling and cursing. The noise startled a flock of birds into the air with a gust of wings. Not knowing why, Donn shouted, "I found it! It's R—" and then the blow sent him into darkness.

When he awoke, he was in a dark cell on a pile of filthy straw. One leg bore a shackle with a chain just long enough for him to touch the bars of the window high on one wall, or the wooden door to his cell. His entire body ached, but it was nothing compared to the pain in his heart. He had failed. Bayn was still trapped, and he was captured.

He hoped they would kill him quickly.

The light of dawn filtered through the barred window, brightened, then faded with night. Donn closed his eyes and sought the oblivion of sleep, but he could not rest.

"I heard your words."

Donn jumped to his feet with a rattle of chains, his heart pounding. The voice...Bayn? Had she been captured too?

"Where are you?" And then he saw a glint of green light at the window. She had not been captured—but how had she managed to reach the prison window? "Did the birds tell you?" He was suddenly aware of how strange that sounded, but somehow he had known when he saw the birds, one different than the others, that Bayn would know what had happened.

A small, soft laugh. "Ah, you see well. Yes, I hear what the birds hear. You found the name?"

"Yes. I tried to say it before they hit me," he said,

moving as close to the window as his chain would allow. "His name is Rieghe."

There was silence, and the green glint vanished for a moment. Then he saw the white flash of her smile from the shadows. "Oh yes. That is the name they obey." She sounded exultant, like she had sighted prey.

"You can leave now?"

"Yes. But do not think I will abandon you—you have given me the key to my freedom, and I will do the same for you. But you must trust me. A shaman could discover your true name, but I cannot. Will you give me a drop of your blood, to be free?"

He could not help laughing. "They plan to take it all in time. Escape, and take one drop with you to freedom."'

"What time remains for you?"

It was actually safer for him now, in the cell. No chance of accidents, and the princes would have spies to watch the spies of the others. "While the king lives, I have time. But I doubt he will see another year."

"I will be swift, then. Hold out your hand." He did, and he felt something sharp prick his finger. The shadow at the window shifted. "I must leave now. I swear by my name, I will return for you and set you free."

"But how..."

Something pale fell through the bars of the window, and he caught it. A feather. He thought he heard the soft beating of heavy wings outside, but it soon disappeared and Bayn did not speak again. She was gone.

He held the feather up to the moonlight. It was white and square-tipped, banded with grey-brown flecks like wood ash. He put it in his pocket with great care.

A month passed with no sign, then two. He had nothing to do but wait and hope. Would she come back? How had she left? What kind of help could she bring that would let him escape as well?

Sometimes he overheard scraps of gossip from the court. The king was now bedridden, and one of the princes had been found dead, probably of poison. The others must think the king would die very soon, then. Occasionally he wondered why he still had hope. When they came at First-snow to tell him of the desert leader, it was almost a relief. He would have something else to think about. But then they took him from the dungeon, and his fragile hope faded away. How could Bayn find him now?

The wedding, by proxy, was to take place tomorrow, on the solstice. Donn stood before the window of his room and glanced at the latch, wondering if he could overcome the wards by throwing himself through the glass. Had even occurred to Tormod he might choose to die, or did he simply not care? He had the horses now. This was Donn's last chance of escaping his fate. The desert people would blind him as soon as he was in their hands.

All was still, the deep azure sky and the moonlit snow, save for one pale shape that beat slowly towards the tower. A familiar shape, of a bird he had seen before. He felt a stir of mild interest as the thing came closer, becoming visible as a great white owl with feathers flecked with grey like wood ash. Closer it came until it fluttered at his window, beating against the panes.

A glimmer of magic washed over the window. When he put his hand against the frame he did not feel the slightest twinge of the wards. Calmly he unlatched the window and opened it wide as the owl glided in on great, soundless wings. He turned to shut the window against the chill.

"A gift for you," said a familiar lilting voice behind him, and he glanced down to see a bone bracelet, carved with runes, that was being offered to him by a white-haired woman with forest-green eyes. Bayn, as she had promised, had returned. "I fear it was a long time in making...but no wall will hold you again."

#

The minor courtier made sure he was present when the castle folk unlocked the door in the morning. He wanted to see the bastard's face, to mock him one last time. There was little else to entertain him these days.

He gaped with the others when they found the casement window opened wide, windblown snow frosting the sill. The room was completely empty—no sign remained of the occupant, no indication of his fate. Some of the assembled company stood frozen in consternation, while the rest were all surprise, wonder, and speculation.

In the midst of the babble the minor courtier stepped to the window, idly noting a small black feather that rocked on the sill, stirred by a tiny breeze. He looked down to the base of the tower and the snow-covered ground below. No crumpled bodies, but he did see the tracks of two large creatures in the snow a short distance away.

"Wolves." He shuddered, and moved away from the window.

CROSSING OVER THE RIVER

The first thing he noticed was the ache, all over, and sharp rocks digging in his ribs. Then light so bright it hammered through his eyelids like a spike until a shadow moved between him and the sun and saved him. Soft, tentative brushes touched his forehead, ear, nose, followed by a gust of warm, grass-scented breath.

Opening his eyes, he saw a hot, cloudless blue sky and a few dusty cottonwoods by a shallow creek. His old buckskin horse Corazon stood next to him, sniffing his face. He'd fallen off again.

"'s all right, girl," Rusty wheezed. "Ain't your fault."

Corazon just whickered and nudged his head with increasing strength until he sat up. That was getting harder and harder to do now. The dull burn in his belly was turning into a coal of fire even whiskey couldn't put out the last few days. Just like the man had said it would.

"Damn sawbones. Why I need some city jimmy tellin' me I'm sick—knew that, that's why I *seen* him! But do I get a fix? Five dollars for nothing!"

Corazon just flicked her ear, having heard about the doctor's many failings before. Rusty looked at his horse. Really looked at her—and saw the hollows in her long face, eyes that weren't any more clear than his, hip bones that stuck out more than they should. He'd done his share of hard living and hell-raising, and Corazon had carried him for much of it. Couldn't just up and abandon her, after all that. Wasn't right.

Man couldn't ask for a better horse. She could side-step the wiliest longhorn like a pretty gal at a dance with five suitors and none to her liking. Never once lost her balance. If ever a horse could get by with just three legs, it would be Corazon.

He had to rest before standing, and rest some more before getting in the saddle again. He'd gone the long way out, hoping to find some stray cattle he could chivvy back to their home ranch for a few dollars, but it was mostly habit and he reckoned his need for pay wasn't near as urgent as his need to find Corazon a place to live out her days when he was gone.

He rode for the nearest town. If it had a name he didn't notice it, or maybe nobody had got around to thinking one up. What buildings it had were scoured bare by dust and wind, but there'd been grand plans at one point, if the peeling sign reading "Grand Opera Coming Soon" was any indication. Rusty watered Corazon and found a place in the shade for her, then went looking.

First place he tried was the feed and farm equipment store, figuring they'd know if anybody did. The oiled-down Percy inside offered him two dollars and mentioned dog food. Rusty left the man curled up on the floor with a broken tooth for that, but he almost fell himself when the pain shot through him from the punch. He didn't have the strength to waste, even if the man had it coming.

Nobody else he could find was much more help, with the exception of the traveling preacher-man sitting outside the saddlery, smoking a pipe while waiting to get his boots repaired.

"I doubt it's what you want to hear, son, but at least the feller wanting her for dog food was honest. There's no other use in an old horse like that. When she ain't being rid, she'll go fast."

Rusty stifled his instinctive curse. "But I got money for her feed! She won't eat much."

"Not what I meant." The preacher knocked the ash from his pipe. "I'm sayin' there are those who will take that money and feed her until you're gone from sight, and then the feedin' will end. That horse will be nothin' special to them, and why should they take the trouble? It's human nature, son. We all fight it, some better'n most."

Rusty thanked him anyway and kept looking. Counting the two gold coins he had stashed in his boot heels for dire emergencies, he had nearly fifty dollars. Ought to be plenty to set an old horse up in style somewhere. Maybe he should move on.

Walking back, the owner of the saddlery waved him over. "That preacher fella remembered something after you left. Said he saw a little farm on the way in, got some pasturage by the river. Might talk to them."

Rusty grunted. "Worth a try, anyway. Where's it at? S'pose I can just follow the river."

"Nah, it's north of the gorge. You head up to that line of hills there, and when you find the rock canyon take that past the gorge. Then you've got the river to take you the rest of the way." Then, as Rusty unhitched Corazon, "You aren't thinking of leaving now? You'll never get there before dark, and you look wore out."

"I am that." Rusty pulled himself up to the saddle with an effort, wincing at the pain. "Lying in a bed won't fix it. Never did get used to sleeping where I can't see the sky, and I don't have the time to work up to it. I'll see this done before I rest."

They moved out at an easy pace toward the hills. Corazon nodded her head as she walked, twitching an ear or grunting in response when he spoke to her. He might have dozed a time or two, trusting to her balance to keep him in the saddle. As the sun sank the heat of the day faded, bringing cool breezes off the hills, and he could hear a coyote yipping far off. When the light was gone completely he made camp.

By now the pain was constant enough sleep was fitful, but each time he started awake he heard the sounds of Corazon shifting her weight or twitching her tail, and he could close his eyes again. You could trust a horse, if you treated it right. More'n a person sometimes. Horses were easier than people for Rusty. They didn't need much to be content, and they let you know if they weren't.

When daylight came he found he could barely move. Even a fire and coffee that was half whiskey didn't help the stabbing pains in his head and belly.

"Just have to get you to that farm, girl," he gasped. "End of the canyon, he said. Nice place by the river. Think you'll like that."

He talked to Corazon like that for hours, as much to keep himself awake as to reassure her. He wasn't seeing right—things would get blurry and the bright sunlight hurt his head. It was harder to sit up in the saddle, too, and he felt himself wobble more than he liked. At some point he'd found the rock canyon and was following it. It didn't seem to be going north, but maybe it would turn in a bit.

Then he lurched hard, and Corazon stumbled. He didn't fall...she'd shifted enough for him to get his balance again, but the jolt of fear burned the fog from his mind. Corazon was limping. She'd hurt herself keeping him safe.

Moving slow and careful, he slid out of the saddle. He'd walk for a bit and give Corazon a rest. He clung to the stirrup and kept going. Even when he saw a big coyote watching them from on top of a cliff. Nothing he could do about it.

At the next turn he saw rock ahead as well as to either side, and he sighed. He was in a box canyon. He'd gone up the wrong one, and Rusty knew in his soul he didn't have the strength to go back and start over. Maybe he could sit and wait for it to get cooler, but there was a good chance he wasn't getting up again if he did.

"Hope you were listening to them directions," he whispered to Corazon. "You get tired waiting for me, go back the way we came and find the river. I'll be along in a bit." There was an old twisted mesquite close to the end of the box canyon. It didn't have much shade but it was better than nothing. He stumbled over, and Corazon followed. He looked at her blearily. That saddle...no need for her to carry that weight now, and the bridle might catch on something. Bad idea with coyotes around.

With his last remaining strength he dragged the saddle and bridle off, then collapsed at the foot of the mesquite. "I'll just...set a while, Corazon. You go on now."

This time, his sleep was restful. Corazon was still there when he awoke, nuzzling his shoulder, and he rubbed his fingers along the edge of her jaw the way she liked. She shifted her head to put another itch in reach. That's when he noticed the ache was gone. Rusty stood and patted her neck, wondering where the mist had come from. Maybe he was closer to the river than he thought.

"Let's find you that farm, girl. It can't be far." He looked about for her tack, not seeing it, then remembered he'd taken it off for good and shrugged. Corazon would follow him without a rope. He did see some large paw prints in the dust, though, and he wondered why a coyote near as big as a wolf wouldn't try his luck with two critters that couldn't much run. Maybe he'd woken up just in time.

Things got blurry and confusing again as he walked. He couldn't seem to find the river no matter how far he went. Sometimes the ground was white like it was covered in snow, but he didn't feel cold. He couldn't remember how long ago it had been since he'd watered Corazon, or eaten anything. He tried heading back to the little town, thinking he could retrace his steps that way, but he couldn't find the town either.

He'd see people up ahead in the mist but they were gone by the time he reached the place he'd seen them. Rusty would have given up a long time ago, but Corazon was still plodding along behind him, following and trusting him to see her safe. So he tried harder. If he ran he could get close enough to see their faces, sometimes. A few would look up when he yelled, but never seemed to want to talk. Just headed off into the fog that never went away.

Odd looking folk, too. Rusty had never seen anybody wearing such strange, short clothes, not outside a bathhouse anyway, and it was all bright colors of the rainbow. One of them half-naked types even seemed to see him, but his eyes went wide and he ran away even faster than he'd come up the trail.

"I'm starting to feel hurt, Corazon. Lord knows I'm no tintype but I ain't *that* ugly, am I? You don't seem to mind none." Corazon snorted.

The fog thickened, then thinned again. Once more Rusty saw someone up ahead, and they were facing away from him. He'd sneak up, then, and get close before they could run.

Seeing trousers he thought they were a boy, but as he got closer he could see long brown hair. At least she was wearing more clothes than the others or he would have been too embarrassed to say anything. She shivered suddenly, rubbing her hands on her arms, and turned her head.

Her mouth fell open, but she didn't run. Rusty was so relieved he felt his knees buckle.

"Ma'am, I'm sorry to trouble you but I'm looking for a farm nearby. Close by the river." She just stared at him, then glanced at Corazon. "Heck, just point me to the river." A worried frown was the only sign on her face. "You speak English? Dammit, I don't have but three words of Spanish and two ain't polite. *Augua?*"

She said nothing, but glanced again at Corazon and even reached out her hand. Then she just...faded. Or the fog came in. He couldn't tell any more. Still, she'd given him a little hope. Maybe the folk here were all deaf, or touched in the head. He just had to keep trying.

The fog thinned a few more times, and he'd see more strange things like lights moving in the sky, or scattered over the valley like all the stars had fallen.

The smell of pork beans wafted past his nose. Rusty stopped, puzzled. He wasn't exactly hungry, but it sure smelled good. And if someone was cooking beans, they'd be likely to stay put for a while. He followed the scent, noticing Corazon had picked up her pace as well.

Up ahead he saw a campfire and a man seated crosslegged on the other side. The fog was hardly visible here, so Rusty could see the man had chosen to build his fire right where two trails crossed. A pot of beans was hanging from an iron tripod over the fire, with a big coffeepot and a tin pieplate of biscuits. A cup, a plate, and a spoon lay on the ground before the fire.

"Come up and help yourself," the man said. "There's plenty. And some sweet grain for your horse."

Considerably astonished, Rusty went up to the fire and sat down. Corazon found the grain and set to, and he served himself a generous portion of fatback and beans.

"Glad to see ya. I've been having the devil's own time out here. Nobody'll talk to me!" Rusty mopped his plate with a biscuit, and poured some coffee. "And here you are, with grub no less. I'm much obliged." He looked at the pot. It seemed just as full as it had been at the beginning, and even though Rusty still held his half-eaten biscuit in one hand the number in the pieplate hadn't changed. He felt a sudden chill.

The man tilted his head, and Rusty saw he had mismatched eyes, one amber brown, the other grey-green. He couldn't place his people, either. Seemed like he could have some Mexican blood, or Indian, or something else Rusty couldn't rightly name. He had black hair hanging about his face, with one lock pale like moonlight.

"I was asked to find you," the man said, gentle-like. "You're lost."

"True enough." Rusty stared at him. "I'm wonderin' how you might know that. That preacher-man send you?"

"My name is Hetchaway. I have a foot in many worlds, and sometimes I can see things others can't. And when people see...lost things, they come to me. Someone told me of seeing an old cowboy with an old horse near here. So, I sent my invitation to find out what troubles you."

Rusty was in deep and dangerous water now, and no mistake. "I have to see to my horse. I don't have long, see, and I was told there was a farm up the river a ways that might take her in. I can't just...leave her." And then all the little things he'd noticed came together sharp and clear. The constant mist, the missing pain. "I'm dead, ain't I."

Hetchaway nodded. "I'm afraid so."

"How long?"

He looked down. "From the looks of you, over a hundred years."

That took some pondering to comprehend. "Then all them people...I was haunting them? That poor girl with the long brown hair...I didn't scare her, did I?"

"She's the one who came to me. She was worried about you both. You seemed tired, she said, and trying to tell her something."

"I was, but she couldn't seemingly hear me. Guess being dead will do that—but how can Corazon be here with me if I'm gone?"

Hetchaway turned his head sharply toward one of the trails, where two pale lights gleamed. Out of the darkness came a big coyote, haunches swaying as it padded forward, completely unafraid of their presence or the fire. It stretched out both forepaws and sank down to the ground, watching Hetchaway with amused interest.

"Old Man knows," Hetchaway sighed, nodding to the coyote. "He says your horse never left you. She died a few days after you did." The coyote yawned, showing sharp white teeth. "His people did not kill her, he saw to that. She went in peace."

"She was staying alive to care for me, just like I was for her," Rusty whispered. "It was all I thought about, at the end. But if we're both dead, what's keeping us?"

Hetchaway spread his hands. "You died with unfinished business, both of you. You're still tied to your bodies, to the earth. I can set you to rest, if I can find you."

Rest sounded really good to Rusty. If he'd been out wandering around for a century or more, that would account for it.

"Trouble is, I wasn't thinking too good at the end. But..." Rust thought hard, trying to remember. "I was looking for a canyon that cut to the river, to the north, and I never found it. What I do remember is a long box canyon with a big ole twisty mesquite near the end." Just saying that, Rusty felt a tug in his chest and a strange certainty filled him. "I think...that's where we are, or pretty near. You'll...we'll be together?"

Hetchaway put his palms together and raised his hands to his forehead. "You will be together. Always."

Rusty stood up and patted Corazon's shoulder, fighting tears. He already felt lighter, like he would blow away in a good breeze. Only one last account to settle, then. "You'll find my things, some of 'em. Reckon the saddle is long gone...but do as you like with 'em. I'm done. 'cept for one last favor I'd ask of you. Had two gold coins in my boots. You give one to that young lady that fetched you, with my apologies. Other'n is yours."

Hetchaway shook his head. "There's no need to pay

me for helping you. I'm glad to do it."

Human nature, the preacher-man had said. Some people fight it better than most, and as far as Rusty could see Hetchaway and the girl had done pretty well. Oughta be helped a bit to encourage 'em, even if he had to be sneaky about it to get around the man's pride.

"Ain't for helping me," Rusty snorted. "It's for helping my horse."

COYOTE AND THE AMAZING
HERBAL FORMULA

One fine spring day Old White Woman was sitting on her porch enjoying a morning smoke. She rocked just enough to make the big wide boards creak like they were talking. The leaves on the trees were budding, and birds flashed by with twigs and grass for nests.

"Somethin' gonna happen," said Old White Woman. She peered up at the sky with one eye, the one that was just a little brighter than the other. "Good. Figger I'm due."

Not long after a figure like a man came staggering down the dirt road from the mountain. He was so dusty a cloud surrounded him as he moved. And what was especially interesting, to Old White Woman's clearest eye, was the dust was grey and the dirt of the road was rusty orange.

"Ooooh," said the stranger. "Water to keep me from crumbling right up in a pile of crumbs. Think of the mess, and me so harmless and weak." He grinned, and collapsed on the steps of the porch.

"Mighty fine teeth you have there. Don't look so weak to me, Tricky One," said Old White Woman. "I got the way of seein' and your tricks don't work on me."

The stranger slumped even further. His head drooped, his ears drooped, and he pretty near drained through the cracks to the ground. "Was it the fur? I'm so weary I could die—which is a thing not so easy for me—and I haven't done what I set out to do." He gave a little howl.

"Don't carry on like that. It ain't fittin' for an old spirit like you. Set you there and I'll fetch some water, and you'll repay me by tellin' me a tale. Ain't heard a new Coyote story since my granny's time."

Old White Woman grabbed her cane, heaved to her feet, and stumped into the cabin. She came back with a tin pitcher of cold well water. Coyote took it and drained the whole thing in one gulp, changing just a bit to stick his snout down inside and lick it dry.

"Brought a little corn squeezin's too. Yer still

droopin' like a chewed string."

Coyote took a swig, wheezed, then took a more respectful sip. "That's the best liquid fire I ever drank, but it's not enough for what ails me."

"And what precisely ails you?" asked Old White Woman. "Yer lookin' pretty hale on the outside."

Coyote reached into his pants and removed his detachable penis. It slumped on the palm of his hand, raw, weeping, and limp as a rotten cucumber.

"Salted green horny toads, that is the saddest peter I ever seen in all my born days," said Old White Woman. Coyote's penis turned its one eye on her and seemed to sigh. "What in tarnation have you been doing with it, diggin' post holes for a five mile fence?"

Coyote gave her a measuring look. "You're closer than you know, you and your seeing eye. I'm grateful for your help, but all I have to offer is a story that is not finished. I'm hoping your wisdom can help me through the other side of it. You see, I've been busy for the last few centuries making love to the Grey Mountain Spirit. She's hard and unyielding and made a bet with me that I could not move her with pleasure. And this," he said, waggling his depressed member, "is the result. I fell asleep at some point. I must go back and win my bet, but how can I with *this*?”

“Oh, I reckon you won, if that’s the mountain in question,” Old White Woman said, pointing with the stem of her pipe back up the road Coyote had traveled. “We don’t get earthquakes much in these parts, so people remember ‘em. Was in my granny’s time. You been sleepin’ a while, Old Man.”

“And I am refreshed!” said Coyote, jumping up. “I am *refreshed*,” he said pointedly to his penis. The penis tried a little hop, and straightened just a bit, then fell and drooped over the sides of Coyote’s hand. “How can you just lie there when I have a debt to pay?” yelled Coyote. “She’s saved us both, you ungrateful lovestick!” The penis just twitched.

“Ain’t interested, thanks all the same. I know where its been,” said Old White Woman.

“I was just thinking, you living all alone and all,” Coyote sulked.

“My man’s been gone ten years now, but we had us a handful a children. Not sayin’ I don’t miss him, and some parts in particular, but I’m set in my ways and I don’t need some wild lover with a tail.”

“Where are these children?” Coyote asked. “They leave you alone here, abandoned? I smell your scent here, but no one else."

Old White Woman snorted. "Abandoned? I talk to 'em alla time. See, while you were sleepin' off yer rock-rubbing we got 'lectricity an' tellerphones and all manner of clever contraptions. My daughter sent me the latest device just last month. A box full of the Innernet! We can send letters and I don't even need to lick a stamp. You can find out most anythin' with that box. It's a marvel."

"You don't say!" said Coyote, greatly impressed. "Do you think it would know how to make this stand up and do its duty?" He waggled the penis again.

"I get messages all the time sayin' they got the stuff ta do it. Come take a look-see."

Coyote followed Old White Woman into the house. Inside was the magic box, which had a glowing window and strange things tied by their tails to the box that made it work. It was exactly as Old White Woman had said. Many, many medicine men claimed to have exactly what was needed to make his manhood harder, longer, wider, more enduring, and remove unsightly back hair. Coyote ignored that part.

"How do I get these medicines?" Coyote asked.

"Sez here you gotta give 'em the numbers offa them

little plastic card things they use for money nowadays. Then they send a package with the medicine to you in the mail."

"But I don't have a plastic card, and mail would take too long. I need a cure now. There's centuries of lovemaking I have to catch up on!"

"You'll be wantin' a softer lover this time, don't forget," said Old White Woman. "Keep on like you've been and you'll break the little guy past fixin'."

Coyote sniffed at the magic box. It had very faint scents, strange and new.

"How do these Internets work, then? How do the messages get in the box?"

Old White Woman shrugged. "It's a mystery to me. All I know, you gotta have that thick string there plugged in just right or it don't work for spit."

Coyote sniffed the wire. The strange scents were stronger there. "I am the best tracker and hunter in the world, am I not? I will track these messages back to where they came from, and ask there for the medicine." He looked at the messages again. One in particular had a scent that made his nose twitch.

"How you gonna fit in that little tiny wire?" Old White Woman asked.

"Shapechanger," Coyote said and smiled, the smile with all the teeth. "I will send you a lover that is not wild and does not have a tail, for you have helped me and I will help you in return." He crouched and sprang into the magic Internet box.

It was very much like swimming in a river of tiny lightning bolts inside the wire, and the river branched so fast Coyote had trouble keeping the scent he wanted.

One of the trails had an end. He poked his head out. A bleary-eyed young man with black hair and a beard sat at a desk with another magic box, staring at him dully. There was a sour smell.

"Is this the place I can find HerbaPotenz?" asked Coyote.

"*Ne,*" said the young man. "This Bulgaria. Get off my screen, dog-faced man. Are you a virus?"

Coyote sniffed, and learned. The young man was something like a trickster, but he did not enjoy his tricks and did them only for power and the numbers on the little plastic cards. Coyote ducked back inside the Internet box, leaving his own trick for the Bulgarian. Now every time he would use his magic box, a picture of a coyote would appear just for a blink and laugh at him.

Coyote found a better track and followed it to

another end. This time when he looked out, there was a woman with big yellow hair and big breasts in a small dress and when she saw him, her eyes became very big too.

"HerbaPotenz is here! I can smell it!" Coyote said. "Look, I need some desperately!" He waved his chapped penis at her.

Big Hair Woman had big, strong lungs too. She screamed and flapped her hands at Coyote, who didn't mind at all because it made her big breasts move like wrestling bear cubs. He jumped out of the magic box to get a better view, but that made Big Hair Woman scream even louder and run away.

"Wait!" called Coyote. "I need the medicine! Where is it?" He ran after her. Now there were lots of screaming and running people. They ran into a big room with a tall roof and many large metal shelves with boxes in them. A big fat man was driving a machine that lifted boxes up and down, but when he saw Big Hair Woman being chased by Coyote he stopped and jumped out. All the people ran out a door that went to the outside. Big Fat Man stopped in the door and faced Coyote. Coyote could smell he was afraid, but he did not move.

"Leave EllaBeth alone! What the hell are you?"

"I just want some HerbaPotenz," Coyote said, "Where can I find some?"

Big Fat Man looked at him suspiciously. "That's all? You're not after EllaBeth?"

Not at the moment, Coyote thought, but he knew better than to say so. "That's all I came here for," he said, opening his eyes wide to look innocent.

"In those boxes, second shelf," Big Fat Man pointed. Coyote ran and jumped up. "No, not that one, it's teeth whitener. You sure don't need that. Other one."

Coyote pulled out a container and opened it. He sniffed. He frowned. "This does not have the power. I smelled it here, and this has much the same scent, but it is not the thing I need."

Big Fat Man scratched his head. "I dunno. I just run the forklift. That's the stuff we send out, but I don't know how it's made. Mister Brett, he might know." He glanced up at some windows that looked down on the big room with the shelves. There was another small room up there, and Coyote could smell an even stronger fear coming from it. He ran up the metal stairs to the small room.

"Are you Mister Brett?" Coyote asked the man hiding under the desk. He had three hairs on top of his head that had been glued in place with strange-smelling fat, and he peeked at Coyote from behind his hands. Three-Hair Man nodded. "I need HerbaPotenz, the real medicine. This is not really HerbaPotenz," Coyote said, tossing the container through the window. Three-Hair Man cringed. "You have it, I smell it on you."

"I used it all!" Three-Hair Man cried. "We changed the formula. It was too expensive to make it like the old guy said. He sent a sample, though, and of course I had to try it, right? It works, so I used it all! We don't have any more!"

"Why don't you ask this medicine man for more?" Coyote asked.

"Well, he'd want to know why we needed it when we told him it wasn't selling," Three-Hair Man said, wriggling uncomfortably. "He's supposed to get a percentage."

"You are making fake medicine and cheating the one who gave it to you?" Coyote growled. "Tell me where to find this man, or I will bite you!"

Three-Hair Man whimpered, and scrabbled at the top of his desk for a big pile of papers. He took one and held it out, shaking. "That's all I have! Now go away!"

"What, no email?" Coyote said, disappointed. He

rather liked using the Internet now.

"He's old; why would he use email?" said Three-Hair Man.

Coyote snarled at him until he curled up in a tight, smelly ball. Then Coyote pinched off a little bit of his shadow and tossed it in the corner, so Three-Hair Man would see it and remember Coyote and always be afraid. Then he set out to find the medicine man.

He followed the address to a big house with many windows, and Coyote was pleased. Only a wealthy medicine man could afford to live in such a big house. Then he smelled that many, many old people lived there. The man he was searching for only lived in a small room, and had very little.

"Are you the one who made the HerbaPotenz?" asked Coyote.

"That is what they are calling it, I am thinking," said Old Medicine Man. "*Mannerwurtzenmittel* was my name for it, but they said nobody could pronounce it and it sounded like something for insects anyway."

Coyote told him his story, including the display of Exhibit P. "Please, can you help me?"

"I believe so," said Old Medicine Man. "I kept a little, for the memories. My dear wife, may she rest in peace, was very fond of it." He took his cane and went to the little cabinet that held his belongings, taking out a fat round glass bottle with a glass stopper.

Coyote caught the scent, and quivered with delight. "That's it!" He took the bottle, pulled the stopper out with his teeth, and poured the medicine over his penis. It bounced up and down, growing stronger and wider with each bounce. Soon it was back to its regular form and ready for action.

"Oooo, I can feel it working. I can't wait to try it out," sighed Coyote. "Now I can have fun again! But before I do—Old Medicine Man, how can I repay you?"

Old Medicine Man smiled sadly. "I always wanted to live in the country, but that would be too much to ask. Perhaps I could move to a room where I could see some trees outside?"

"How about a whole forest, with a mountain? Possibly even a nice older lady to love? I do *not* mean the mountain." Coyote put the medicine bottle back in his hand. "You may need this." He lifted the Old Medicine Man into the chair with wheels and ran to the big room where all the people met, for he had seen a magic Internet box there. "We'll just make a few stops on the way."

Coyote jumped into the magic box, holding Old Medicine Man close. He remembered one of the tricks the Bulgarian had, and he could use it to trick Three-Hair Man into giving up the money he owed. The magic box, as Old White Woman had said, was indeed powerful. He could even go to the machines where the money came out, because they were also connected to the lightning river like the magic boxes.

And so it was Old White Woman saw Old Medicine Man suddenly appear in her house, a glass bottle in his hand and his pockets full of money. He looked very confused.

"I am apologizing for the intrusion, but there was this...person, and he—"

"Don't tell me. Lots of teeth, kinda hairy around the edges?"

Old Medicine Man nodded.

"Why don't you just set a while and tell me all about it. I do love a good story," said Old White Woman.

INSCRIPTION

I wish there were another way to do this. You didn't have any warning and now I've changed your life, just by writing the words you are reading. Your situation won't get much worse if you read the rest, though, so if you can do so without getting caught, I'll try to explain. It might help you survive.

My name is Dexon, and I worked in this Complex for ten years. My Social Index was never high enough for any of the sealed urbs, and I'm guessing you have the same problem or you wouldn't be here. And obviously they never fixed the leak or you wouldn't have found this message. Try unclogging the drain first.

It started like this.

I was crouched in a dusty corridor, hastily eating

some stale protein chips I'd stolen and trying to figure out a solution to an increasingly desperate problem that could get me killed, when I noticed the smell of mold, old and sour. I felt a stab of fear—if the safety committee found mold our team would get a toxic health hazard fine, and I was dangerously close to permanent reassignment as it was. Of course the monitors claim they want us to have a healthy work environment, even if they won't give us the equipment we need to actually do work.

So I did everything a good Mindful Citizen should do—signed out a set of safety gear on my task pad and went to fix the problem before they noticed anything. I put down "repair work" as the reason. That was vague enough to cover anything I needed to do and I knew the safety committee monitored equipment usage. I was supposed to be doing cleaning and maintenance anyway so it was approved immediately.

The smell was strongest in a section of the Complex that had been built before the Fourth War, possibly before the Third. They used a strange, compressed chalky substance sandwiched between thin sheets of fiber for interior walls back then. I pulled away furniture and storage cabinets until I saw it—a mottled black stain spotting the surface near the concrete floor. The chalky part of the wall had turned to a slimy, sticky mess, but I eventually got enough pulled free to see something was blocking a drain. It looked like a pile of large leaves, and I was surprised when they came out all together, as if they were attached.

The leaves were rectangular, and had writing on them, most of it still legible. Not interactive like a task pad, just marks on the surface, and I wondered how it had been done. Reading further I figured out this thing was called a *magazine*. One article was titled, *How to make a pencil—what we don't know about technology.* If you are unfamiliar with the term, a pencil is a device that makes marks, for writing, but doesn't use electronics. So it can't be traced. Ever. And it can be erased, too.

You can see why I thought this might be useful.

Enough of the article was legible to let me know I needed wood, graphite, and clay. I think it was the mention of wood that really started me thinking. It wouldn't be enough to just have something to write with; it would need to be easily concealable too, and I had an idea. I picked greenspace cleanup for my mandatory volunteer hours that week. The greenspace here is large enough that no matter where the job router defined my section, there would be some kind of shrub in reach. Then I saved a handful of dead branches of the right thickness and brought them back in with me. Not something you could hide, and I didn't try. I put them in an old metal container I'd found elsewhere in the Complex, made a few "leaves" from broken circuitboard and put it in the Mindfulness niche of my personal space. The Social Index evaluator gave me so many biopoints my index actually went up.

Graphite I tracked down in the lubricants cabinet, strangely enough. It's used where volatile hydrocarbons would contaminate a processor, or to gain biopoints for the Complex. Clay was much more difficult. Eventually I went back to where I had found the mold and used the chalky white powder from the old interior wall. Then it was just a matter of drilling a long, thin hole down the center of a piece of branch and carefully packing it with a paste made from the graphite and powder, mixed with a little water. Since my "pencil" still looked like a piece of branch, I could hide it with the other branches in the niche and no monitor would even think to examine it. They had approved of it earlier, after all.

Of course I needed something to write on, too. Something easily hidden, or that could be mistaken for something else. It would be dangerous to leave a message where the monitors might find it. One of the processors on the lower level makes big sheets of plastic film—they use it in the urbs, I have no idea what for—and the trimmer leaves odd bits and pieces behind. Dipped in microchip rinse solution, the film becomes frosted and rough enough for the pencil to work, and with a little effort it looks just like a piece of beancake wrapper. Another thing the monitors wouldn't notice.

Have you noticed yet how freeing this message is? I'm communicating with you, directly, without any evaluator program involved. No monitoring. *No one else knows.* It's just like the bird...no, I'll explain the bird later. I can say whatever I want here, and just to you. They had a word, long ago, to describe this. I read it in another part of that magazine I found. *Private.*

This message is a permanent record of my thoughts, but independent of me. I could even be dead by now, but my words still live in your mind as you read them. I didn't go to all this effort for you, of course. I don't know who you are. Certainly I wouldn't risk erasing my entire Social Index and reassignment to a permanent punishment post for a stranger.

I did it for Jessen.

She arrived at the Complex three years ago, just in time. I was almost completely broken at that point. They never fed us enough—hence the stolen protein chips—and I didn't have enough Index points to earn even the lowest comfort privileges. In other Complexes I had been able to find some way to get enough extra points for stimulants or entertainment tokens, even though I wasn't very good at pretending to think like a model Mindful Citizen. Not here. The monitors only cared about meeting production goals, and when we couldn't do it everyone got fined. How that was supposed to fix broken equipment was never clear to me, but that's the monitors for you. I was barely staying ahead of the fines to keep my minimum index score above the punishment detail level. It wasn't that I wanted to die, but I didn't really want to live either.

The remote monitor actually came online and spoke to us personally at assembly to tell us Jessen had volunteered in order to "re-dedicate her commitment to being a Mindful Citizen and to work on improving the community service component of her Index." Jessen stood in front of the assembly, her expression as empty as ours were and her eyes humbly downcast, but I saw her chin lift up just a little at those words, the muscles in her jaw tense. Not enough for the monitor to notice, fortunately, but it was as good as a shout to a fellow rebel like me. Somebody else was fighting, and seeing it gave me strength to keep fighting too.

Then I noticed...little things. A "good day" used to be getting fresh beancake instead of old, rancid stuff, but now it was a day when I saw Jessen. Or heard her voice. Or even saw her name on the duty roster. It meant she was still here at the Complex, still alive. Everything about her was mysterious and wonderful to see, even the faint freckles just under her grey-green eyes, or the way her sandy hair curled under at the end except for one stubborn strand. Her very existence made my burdens easier to bear. And sometimes, when our eyes briefly met, I could almost imagine a trace of emotion there. That maybe, possibly, she was glad to see me too.

Of course as soon as I realized what had happened I panicked. If anyone had noticed, had thought I had committed any of the Unwelcome Behaviors, the fine would be large enough to zero out the social component of my Index. I didn't think I had, but you know that's no excuse. I struggled for over a year, even thought about how I could improve my Index to the point where I could petition for contact—but she might say no. I couldn't be sure. Also, the things I wanted to say, to ask, were too dangerous to be said in the presence of the Safe Contact monitor.

Then I tried to find a way to communicate with her that the evaluator programs wouldn't see. But everything is watched, every means of communication that uses the network. Our task pads sound an alert if they get too close to one another, and an automatic investigation is started. Any job requiring more than one person is monitored, and non-essential conversation fined. We only meet in groups for assembly, and that is monitored too. Our personal spaces are sealed at curfew, and the viewscreens check that you are present for the daily lecture then. I couldn't find a solution.

But then I found the magazine with the pencil article. I was desperate enough to try anything to make contact with Jessen. If I could do it in a way that wouldn't put her in danger...then I would know. She would know. It was worth the risk. Oh, don't shake your head. I hope you find someone someday that will be worth the risk to you.

My desperation was fueled by a fortunate but temporary circumstance. In the usual quarterly randomization of personal spaces, Jessen had been assigned the space next to mine. Knowing she was so close, and yet still out of reach—well, those were some very long nights. I could hear her move about, hear the creak of her bed, even, sometimes, her breathing. *And I could not speak.* The end of the quarter would move her away again. I was desperate to do something, *anything*, to end the agony.

I wrote a message. Short but to the point. "Want to communicate? Make a hole in this if you do." It's easy for me now but then I had to struggle to remember what letters looked like on a screen and then make them with this rough twig with a dark tip instead of a keypad. I rolled up the plastic film, tied it to the end of a long string with a metal washer at the end for weight, and when the lights dimmed for sleep cycle, I shoved it between the ceiling tiles and the wall divider with another section of branch until it dangled on her side of the wall.

My heart was pounding so hard I felt dizzy. Had the monitors heard the noise? Had Jessen seen the note? Would she understand what I was trying to do? I felt a small tug on the string I was holding in my sweaty hand, and I could barely breathe. She might denounce me. She might be afraid to reply. I had done all that I could do.

After an eternity I felt a stronger tug on the string, and I slowly pulled it back. The plastic looked a bit odd in the dim light, and when I unrolled it I saw why. Jessen had *bitten* a hole in the film. Savagely.

I took that as a "yes."

Over the next few days I sent her some pieces of plastic film and a pencil. We ended up just leaving our messages in the space above the ceiling tiles, always when the lights were dimmed. By the time our spaces were moved apart we had figured out other safe places to leave messages. Since we had a way to communicate that the evaluators couldn't detect, we could also figure out places to meet in person, during the work day. No, we didn't find a way to turn off the task pad proximity sensors. We didn't need to. In the better-maintained Complexes you are required to keep them in physical contact if you aren't in your personal space or it sets off another alarm, but here they had to turn that off because we are constantly repairing equipment in tight spaces and task pads are expensive to replace. This place also doesn't have surveillance everywhere, because of all the old, strange buildings they enclosed in the Complex. If it was clear of sensors, we'd leave our pads in our duty areas and the monitors never knew we had moved away from them.

At first we didn't dare spend more than a few minutes together, and we'd only speak in hushed voices, but it was worth it. Worth it to actually touch another human being, even if briefly. I didn't dream about escaping by dying any more. I dreamed about Jessen and the way her warm breath traced across my cheek when she whispered in my ear, the scent of her hair, the comforting sensation of her hand entwined in mine. When the rations were short I would remember things she had said, her fleeting smile, and hunger felt less sharp.

Even the writing itself was a strange pleasure. I had not realized the act of creating letters by hand would be so individual, but Jessen's writing was as distinctive and recognizable as her voice. Although we usually erased old messages, for security and to reuse the film, I kept the little slip where she first wrote "I love you," because it was like keeping her by me even in the days we couldn't see each other. Days of separation built on each other to create an unbearable ache, so we found ways to stay together longer when we did meet. Which created a new set of problems, and the reason you are reading this.

We didn't have any plans then. We were barely

staying alive. Free, unmonitored communication was new and overwhelming, and so was physical contact. I suppose we thought we would eventually be discovered and it wouldn't matter in the end. We didn't think about survival, just getting one more moment together. We got better at it, using the system of isolation for our own purposes. I guess we became overconfident, and as I said, we weren't thinking very far ahead.

We were good at hiding, after living all our lives in this world you are still, for now, a part of. But some things can't be hidden. At first it didn't make sense when she told me. I guess I thought pregnancy could only happen from a Sanctioned Contact. I remember how at first I felt completely numb. I was going to die. They would know. Jessen would be taken away from me. Then I realized someone else would be taken away, and I was filled with a cold fear and determination I've never felt before in my life.

Everything that had once been important changed in an instant. All the old excuses I had used before vanished. Jessen and the baby had to live, and I would do whatever was necessary to make that happen. Now I had a reason to fight, something to fight for. I knew what my decision meant. We could not live in the Complex, which left only one option. We had to go into the Waste.

It terrified me, but we had no choice. We couldn't stay—and even if what they said about the Waste was true at least we would die together. We had to leave so our child would even have a chance to live. We would use violence, yes, and even kill to do this. I don't expect you to understand, not yet. I wouldn't either in your situation. Just remember what I have told you, and there will come a time when you will.

We didn't have much time—Jessen figured maybe a month before it became noticeable. Our messages now were all about finding food and supplies to take with us, hiding the fact these things were missing until we were gone, caching everything where we could grab it quickly and without detection. With my maintenance job I had the perfect excuse to go all over the Complex, looking for a way out that wasn't watched—and I found it. They tried to seal the joins between the old buildings when they built this Complex, but they didn't always do a good job—or check the old buildings completely. I found a hatch that led to a hidden part of a roof, and from there, a series of ladders and bricked-off balconies that went all the way to the ground. I'll try to cover our tracks so they won't find it when we're gone. Might be useful to you.

That reminds me...the roof is where I saw the bird. Sure, you've seen pictures, maybe even a brief video, but that isn't anything like seeing them in flight. They keep them out of the greenspace somehow, maybe a mesh net. I'm beginning to think that's another thing they do to keep us from getting ideas.

See, the ability to fly requires the freedom to fall. Shield someone from any possibility of harm and there is no chance of joy. Sometimes the birds swoop and dive for no reason I could see, maybe just for fun. Because they can. The monitors say we must be watched so we can't say or do anything harmful to each other. Maybe so, but what do they allow us to say that has meaning? No one else needs to hear me tell Jessen I love her. The only permission I need is hers. They won't let us fall, but we aren't allowed to fly either.

By this time we will have left the Complex, one way or another. I don't know what they are saying about us; traitors, selfish anti-social bigots, individualist saboteurs? Or have they made no mention of our crimes at all, afraid that even mentioning them would create more rebels?

You're one of us now, whether you want it or not.

Unsanctioned thoughts are in your mind. Dangerous information in your memory. You can turn this message in if you want, but it won't save you. Your Social Index is gone once they find out, never to return. Destroy this if you must; there are others hidden where the monitors will not find them. You can try to go back to your life in the Complex, try to live like you did before, if you can call that living. It's your choice. I don't think you will. It only takes one taste to realize how *hungry* you are for real human contact. For communication. For touch. It's worth it. Worth escaping. I'm not going to write down how I figured it out, just in case they do find this, but all the stories the monitors have told us about the Waste being impossible to live in? Lies. *More* lies. I've already been outside the Complex, and returned unharmed.

When you decide to leave, write your own message for those who follow. Tell them your story, help them escape. Leave a record that will outlive you. Come and find us, and discover what happened after I sealed this message for you to read.

Don't be afraid. You already know how to hide to survive, and now you have something to live for.

And I left you a pencil.

ABOUT THE AUTHOR

Sabrina Chase was originally trained as a Mad Scientist, but due to a tragic lack of available lairs at the time of graduation fell into low company and started working in the software industry. She lives in the Pacific Northwest and is owned by two cats.

Further sordid details may or may not be available at her website, chaseadventures.com